TRIPLE HEADER

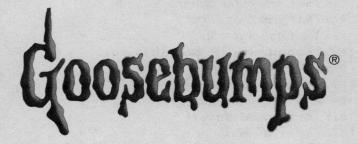

R.L. STINE

THREE SHOCKING TALES OF TERROR

—— Book 1 ——

Look for more Goosebumps books
by R.L. Stine:
(see back of book for a complete listing)

TRIPLE HEADER

Goosebumps®

R.L. STINE

THREE SHOCKING TALES OF TERROR

—————— Book 1 ——————

AN
APPLE
PAPERBACK

SCHOLASTIC INC.
New York Toronto London Auckland Sydney

A PARACHUTE PRESS BOOK

ISBN 0-590-35007-2

12   11   10   9   8   7   6   5   4   3   2   1   7 8 9/9 0 1 2/0

Printed in the U.S.A.   40

First Scholastic printing, October 1997

Contents

Welcome to Triple Terror

SLIM: Hello, hello, hello, boys and ghouls. Welcome to the first *Goosebumps Triple Header.* I'm a triple header too. My name is Slim. I'm the good-looking one between these two ugly geeks.

LEFTY: I'm the one with all the brains.

RIGHTY: How many brains do you have now?

LEFTY: Twelve.

RIGHTY: Is *that* what's in your lunch box?

LEFTY: Hey — don't *you* eat them. They're mine!

SLIM: Don't fight, guys. I'll slap you both black and blue!

RIGHTY: Promise?

LEFTY: Me first.

SLIM: Don't pay any attention to those

losers, boys and ghouls. They're jealous because I look so much like Brad Pitt.

LEFTY: You don't look like Brad Pitt. You look like an *arm*pit!

RIGHTY: You look like what *grows* in an armpit!

SLIM: Let's stop complimenting each other and get to our stories. Each *Goosebumps Triple Header* has three stories. That means *three times* the scares. I hope you'll collect them all.

LEFTY: All you collect is *dust*!

SLIM: Sigh . . . whoever said that three heads are better than two?

Ghost Granny

Introduction

SLIM: Any of you guys seen Granny?

LEFTY: I saw her this morning. She looked okay.

RIGHTY: Too bad she's dead.

LEFTY: She's dead? Wow. I *thought* she'd been awful quiet for the last year!

SLIM: Maybe we should take her out of the kitchen and bury her in the backyard.

LEFTY: No way! I don't want to smell up the backyard!

SLIM: Well, *Ghost Granny* is the name of our first story. It's about a girl named Kelly who is being haunted by her own granny. Granny Deaver is dead and buried. So why is her ghost hanging around the house, howling till all hours of the night? How do you get rid of a ghost that's ruining your life?

3

RIGHTY: When you readers find out, *you'll* howl too!

LEFTY: I like this story. It stays with you — like a really good skin rash.

SLIM: I give it six thumbs-up!

1

I know it's wrong to hate someone in your own family. But the truth is, we *all* hated Granny Deaver.

She wasn't our real grandmother. She was a friend of our grandmother's sister. She came to visit us one day — and never left!

She stayed for three years. I feel terrible for saying it. But she totally ruined our lives.

I sat across from her at every dinner. She slurped her soup and let it run down her chin. She clicked her teeth and burped really loud.

My brother, Jeff, sat next to her. She liked to grab food off his plate and gobble it down before he could complain. Sometimes she used his napkin to blow her nose.

"Kelly, you eat like a bird," she would say to me. Then she would pinch my arm so hard, I'd

5

scream. "Put some meat on your bones!" Granny Deaver would cry. Then she would cackle her head off, as if that was a really funny joke.

She was always sneaking up behind Jeff and me and pinching us. She loved to pinch the backs of our necks. Once, she pinched my arm so hard, I started to bleed!

We tried to be nice to her. But she never stopped complaining.

"Is this vegetable soup or dirty dishwater?" she would ask. She slurped it down, making horrible sucking sounds. And she complained about every spoonful.

She always complained if someone got a bigger portion than she did. Sometimes she would grab food off our plates and feed it to her cat.

Sammy, her cat, was more horrible than Granny Deaver.

The cat liked to scratch our legs with his sharp claws. When he wasn't scratching us, the cat took his claws to the furniture. If we tried to pet him, he would bite us.

Sammy constantly missed the cat box. And he was always coughing up disgusting things. Granny Deaver refused to clean up after him. So Jeff and I had to do it all.

Luckily, Sammy ran away one day and never came back.

But we were stuck with Granny Deaver.

At breakfast, she drank the milk right from the carton. One morning, her teeth fell into the carton and she kept right on drinking.

After that, Jeff and I gave up cereal.

Whenever my friends came over, Granny Deaver would sit in the middle of the room and cackle so loud, we couldn't talk. If I led my friends to another room, Granny Deaver would follow us.

I had no privacy. I had no life.

One day, Granny Deaver wiped her mouth on the silk-screen art project I'd spent weeks on. "That's an art project?" she cried. "It looked like a napkin!"

I went storming in to Mom and Dad. "I can't take it anymore!" I screamed. "She's horrible! Horrible! Why does she have to live with us?"

Mom raised a finger to her lips. "Kelly — she'll *hear* you!" she scolded.

"I don't care!" I shrieked. "I can't take it anymore!"

Dad lowered his newspaper and shook his head sadly. "I feel the same way," he told me. "But what can we do? She's an old woman. And she has nowhere else to go."

"But — but —" I sputtered, holding up my ruined silk screen. "She's not related to us. She moved in here, and now she acts as if she's the queen of everyone!"

"We're her only family," Mom said softly. "We can't just toss her out on the street."

"Why not?" Jeff grumbled.

"Because we're nice people," Dad replied. "We believe in doing what's right."

"Aaaaagh!" I let out an angry cry and shook my fists at the ceiling.

It was no use arguing with my parents. We'd had the same conversation a million times. They were as helpless as Jeff and I.

What could we do?

I turned and stormed up to my room. To my surprise, I found Granny Deaver in my clothes closet.

"What are you doing in here?" I demanded.

I gasped when I saw that she had pulled my clothes off the hangers and tossed them on the floor.

"My closet is too small," she grumbled. "Come in here and help me hang my clothes in your closet."

I wanted to scream. I wanted to cry.

I wanted to pick up the bony old woman all by myself and heave her out the front door.

Imagine how strange I felt when she died that night.

2

Jeff and I had never been to a funeral before.

The funeral parlor was dark and cold and gloomy. Even the flowers Mom and Dad bought didn't brighten it up.

The four of us sat on a hard bench in the front row. Behind us, an old man played slow, sad music on an organ.

No one else came to Granny Deaver's funeral. She didn't have any friends. She almost never went out of our house. So no one else in town knew her.

I stared up at the dark wood coffin. Dressed in her best black dress, Granny Deaver lay on her back with her arms at her sides.

Her silvery hair was neatly brushed. Her eyes were closed. Her cheeks were rosy red.

I stared hard at her. Was it really Granny Deaver? When she was alive, she was always so pale and yellow.

The organ music grew louder. Then it stopped. A man in a black suit stepped up beside the coffin. He asked us to bow our heads in prayer.

I bowed my head. I tried to feel sad.

I know that you are supposed to feel sad at a funeral.

But I couldn't.

Mom and Dad sat silently with their heads bowed and their hands in their laps. Beside me, Jeff fidgeted and coughed.

I knew they didn't feel sad, either.

Staring down at the floor, I had some pretty strange thoughts.

It was just like Granny Deaver to die *two days* before my birthday, I thought bitterly. She was always ruining everything.

I wondered if Mom would still let me have my party. Or if we would have to be in mourning or something.

I didn't feel like mourning. I know it's a terrible thing to say. But as the sad organ music started up again, I wanted to sing and dance and jump for joy.

*   *   *

We were all feeling pretty giddy at dinner. Mom and Dad kept humming some silly song I'd never heard before. We all laughed like crazy when Jeff's spaghetti kept falling off his fork.

Finally, he picked up a long strand between his fingers and slowly sucked it into his mouth. Usually, Mom or Dad would give him a hard time for being such a slob.

But tonight it was funny. Tonight *everything* was funny.

We all felt so good. So cheerful.

I felt as if our family was back. We couldn't be ourselves while Granny Deaver was here. We could never act natural.

But now we were back. And it felt so great.

Mom scooped out big bowls of chocolate ice cream for dessert. We started to eat it. And all four of us burst out laughing — for no reason at all.

It was the happiest night I could remember in a long, long time. Later, as I lay in bed trying to fall asleep, I realized I still had a smile on my face.

I finally drifted off at eleven or so. But I didn't sleep for long.

I woke up suddenly — and glanced at my clock radio. Twelve twenty.

I heard a banging noise from downstairs.

11

Soft thuds.

The sounds must have awakened me.

Is someone walking around down there? I wondered. Who could be awake this late?

Yawning, I lowered my feet to the floor. And listened.

More soft, thudding footsteps.

It might be Jeff, I decided. He ate way too much ice cream and then complained that he had a stomachache.

I pulled my nightshirt down and made my way to the hallway.

Leaning on the banister, I crept down the stairs.

I heard a cough. A bump.

Yes. Someone was in the kitchen.

I tiptoed through the dining room and stopped at the entrance to the kitchen. The lights were all off. Someone was moving around in the darkness.

"Jeff?" I called, my voice hoarse from sleep. "Is that you?"

I clicked on the light.

"Granny Deaver!"

3

The rosy red color had faded from her cheeks. As she smiled at me, her skin was a sickly green. And her tiny eyes had sunk back into her eye sockets.

"I'm back!" she declared in a throaty whisper.

"But — but —" I stuttered, my whole body stiff with horror.

"I couldn't stay away," Granny Deaver whispered, smiling with peeling blue lips. "Too much to do."

Before I could back away, she rushed at me. She threw her bony green arms around me, trying to hug me.

So cold . . . her arms were so cold.

I could barely feel them as they wrapped

13

around my shoulders. I felt only a rush of cold air. Cold, sour air.

I shivered and uttered a sick cry.

As Granny Deaver floated back, I heard another cry — from behind me.

I spun around to see Jeff, followed by Mom and Dad. Their mouths were open in horror. Their eyes bulged.

"She — she's back," I choked out, pointing to the ghostly green form that hovered in front of me.

"Noooooo!" Mom wailed.

Dad grabbed Mom's shoulder. I couldn't tell if he was trying to calm her down or hold himself up.

"I — I can see right *through* her!" Jeff stammered in a tiny voice.

And then he let out a scream as Granny Deaver reached out to pinch his cheek.

Her fingers cracked as she tried to clamp them onto Jeff's skin.

Jeff's knees buckled, and he collapsed to the floor.

Granny Deaver tossed her head back in a whispery cackle. Her tiny eyes rolled wildly in the gaping eye sockets.

"Wh-what are you doing here?" Mom finally choked out.

Granny Deaver floated off the floor. "I came back," she whispered. "I didn't want you to miss me."

"But you — you —" Mom's words caught in her throat.

"Go on back to sleep," Granny Deaver ordered. "I'll keep my old room in the attic. It's cramped and it's drafty. But I don't care. I'm dead, anyway."

I felt another gust of cold, sour air as she moved past me. We all turned and gaped in horror as she floated up the stairs.

"It — it's *impossible*!" Jeff declared, shaking his head.

Dad nodded. "Yes. It *is* impossible." He swallowed hard. "But we *saw* her. We saw her and we heard her. She's back. Granny Deaver is back."

"She's dead and she's back," Mom murmured, her expression dazed.

"What are we going to do?" I wailed.

"I'm . . . frightened," Jeff admitted. "I . . . I'm really frightened."

"We're all frightened," Dad replied.

"But what are we going to do?" I repeated frantically.

Mom rubbed her temples with her fingertips. She always does that when she has one of her headaches. "It's too late. I can't think clearly," she said.

"But — but —" I sputtered.

"Your mom is right," Dad agreed, sliding his arm around her waist. "We're all too shocked and frightened. We can't come up with a plan tonight."

"But she's up in the attic!" Jeff cried, raising his eyes to the ceiling.

"There's nothing we can do tonight," Dad said. "Let's all go to sleep. We can talk about what to do about her tomorrow."

"But tomorrow is my birthday party!" I wailed.

Dad narrowed his eyes at me. I could see that he had forgotten all about my party.

But I hadn't. Eight of my friends were coming over in the afternoon. I couldn't have a birthday party with a cackling old ghost floating around!

"Don't worry, Kelly," Mom said. "She'll be gone by your party."

"Right," Dad agreed.

"How do you know that?" I demanded.

"She can't stay here," Mom replied. "She's a ghost. She has to move on to . . . to wherever ghosts go. Right?"

"Right," Dad agreed again. I think Dad was

so shook up, he would agree to *anything* Mom said!

"Do you *promise* she won't spoil my party?" I demanded.

Mom and Dad exchanged glances. "Let's talk about it in the morning," Mom said. "We'll figure out what to do. I know we will."

Mom gave Jeff a hug. She guided him to the stairs. "Let me tuck you in."

"Do I have to sleep in my room?" Jeff asked in a tiny voice.

"You'll be okay in your room. She won't hurt you," Mom told him. "It's only Granny Deaver, after all."

But she's a ghost now. How do you know she hasn't changed? I thought to myself. But I didn't say it out loud.

I climbed into bed and pulled the covers up over my chin. I knew I'd never get to sleep. My whole body was still shaking. My blood pulsed against my temples.

A ghost, I thought.

We have a ghost in our house.

And not just any ghost. The ghost of Granny Deaver.

Will she be as gross and unpleasant as she was when she was alive? I wondered as I gazed up at the ceiling.

17

I gripped the edge of the blankets tightly with both hands.

Will she stay and stay and stay? And ruin our lives forever?

She can't! I told myself. She's dead. She can't stay. She doesn't belong here anymore.

With these thoughts whirling around in my brain, I finally fell asleep.

But a short while later, I was awakened by the brush of a cold hand against my cheek.

4

"**J**eff—?" I whispered. I sat up, blinking. "Jeff? Is that you?"

I felt the cold touch on my cheek again. And squinted into the pale green face of Granny Deaver.

I opened my mouth to scream — but no sound came out.

I gaped at her in horror. "What do you want?" I finally managed to whisper.

"I can't sleep," she croaked. The tiny, sunken eyes locked on mine.

"Maybe the dead don't sleep." She sighed. "Maybe I'll never sleep again. You'll stay awake and keep your old granny company, won't you?"

She tried to pinch me. Her fingers made a sick, cracking sound, as if her hand was falling apart.

But I couldn't even feel the pinch.

I felt only a brush of cold.

"We'll have a nice chat," Granny Deaver said, floating above me. "Your room is so much more comfortable than mine, Kelly. So much warmer. Now that I'm dead, I don't know if I want to stay up in the attic. Maybe I'll move in with you."

"Ohhhh." I couldn't help it. I tried to hold it in. But a horrified moan escaped my throat.

Granny Deaver didn't seem to hear it. "Now that I'm dead," she continued, "I need to stay closer to the living." She pressed against me. Tried to give me a hug.

My stomach lurched. I swallowed hard. I thought I was going to toss my dinner.

Cold, sour-smelling air wrapped around me. I shivered. I couldn't stop shivering.

She fluttered away, vanishing for a moment into the darkness of my room. Then she shimmered back into view.

"I met the nicest people in the cemetery." Granny Deaver sighed. "All dead. Of course."

I gripped the edge of the blankets tighter and squinted through the darkness at her. Why was she telling me all this? Did she really plan to stay up talking all night?

Granny Deaver tsk-tsked. She bit her peeling lips. "I never believed in ghosts," she said. "I mean, who in her right mind believes in ghosts? But I do now."

She shifted in midair. "Oh, I did meet some ugly ghosts in the cemetery. You and your brother aren't exactly the greatest-looking people in the world. But believe me, Kelly — you're a beauty compared to them. These ghosts were *ugly* with a capital *Ugh*."

"Thanks a bunch," I muttered under my breath.

"They were falling apart," Granny Deaver continued. "Just falling apart, piece by piece."

She shook her head, frowning. "I said to them, 'Listen to me. Just because you're dead, you shouldn't stop worrying about your appearance.'"

She sighed again. "But they were all so nice. Such good new friends. That's the thing about dead people. They stick together. And they stick up for each other."

She floated higher until she was staring down at me from the ceiling. "Look. I'm flying. Like Peter Pan. I never could stand that sappy play."

She shut her eyes. Her face glimmered

green in the pale light from outside the window. "What was I talking about? Oh, yes. My new friends in the cemetery."

She floated closer to me, so close I felt the cold wind on my face.

"Are you listening to me?" she demanded angrily. "A person is dead here. How about a little respect?"

"Of course I'm listening," I choked out. "I'm . . . frightened. I'm sorry. But you're really scaring me."

She turned away from me. "I can take a hint. Even a ghost can tell when she isn't wanted."

"Sorry," I murmured again. I didn't know what to say.

Finally, she floated out the door. "Pleasant dreams," she whispered. But she didn't say it sweetly. She said it bitterly.

She vanished out the door.

I sank back on my pillow and shut my eyes. The clock radio read 2:45 in the morning.

I tried desperately to fall asleep. I didn't want to sleepwalk through my birthday party the next afternoon.

But as soon as I started to drift off, a loud howl made me sit straight up.

"Huh?" I gasped.

Another long, frightening howl rose up from somewhere above my head.

The attic.

Another low moan rising to a screeching cry.

Granny Deaver is howling up there, I realized. Howling at the top of her lungs. Howling like a ghost.

I dropped back onto the bed and covered my head with the pillow.

Another long, mournful howl.

I pressed the pillow harder over my face, over my ears.

"What am I going to do?" I wondered out loud.

"I can't take this. I can't! What am I going to do?"

5

I hurried down to breakfast, eager to discuss the Granny Deaver problem with my family. But the horrible old ghost was already seated at the breakfast table when I came into the kitchen.

Jeff sat across from her, glumly staring down at his scrambled eggs. I saw that he hadn't taken a bite.

Mom and Dad stood side by side in front of the kitchen counter. They both looked pale and tired. Mom had her nervous eye twitch back. She hasn't had it in years.

"These eggs are too runny," Granny Deaver complained. She moved a fork through the eggs on her plate. She tried raising a forkful to her mouth. But the eggs went right through her green skin.

"Runny, shmunny," she muttered bitterly. She dropped her fork onto the plate. "What difference does it make? I can't eat. Do you believe it? The dead aren't allowed to eat. Is that fair?"

She shoved her plate away from her. "Enjoy your breakfast, everyone," she said sarcastically. "Enjoy it while you can."

She motioned for me to sit down. "Come on, Kelly. Have some eggs. You eat like a bird. Come on. Don't just stand there gawking as if you've seen a ghost."

She cackled. "Did I just make a joke?" she exclaimed. "See? I'm dead, but I'm still joking. That's what I call spirit." She cackled some more. A disgusting sound, like dry coughing.

She sighed. "A lot of good it does me. I can't even eat one of your disgusting, runny eggs."

I glanced at Mom and Dad. They lowered their eyes to the floor.

Reluctantly, I took a seat next to Jeff. "How are you doing?" I whispered. "You okay?"

He shrugged.

"No whispering!" Granny Deaver declared. "No secrets, you two." Her eyes had sunk even farther into her skull. Her upper lip had completely fallen off.

"You were talking about me — weren't

you?" she accused Jeff and me. "What were you saying about me, Kelly?"

"Uh . . . nothing," I replied softly. "I just said good morning."

Granny Deaver humphed. "You say good morning to your wimpy little brother, but you don't say good morning to someone who has just died?"

"Good morning," I said. And then I blurted out, "Why were you howling like that all night?"

The old ghost shrugged her bony shoulders. "Beats me," she replied. "I guess I was bored."

"But it was too loud!" I complained. "I didn't sleep all night!"

"There you go again," Granny Deaver replied, rolling her tiny eyes. "Only thinking of yourself. Stop being so selfish, Kelly. Why don't you stop to think about me once in a while?"

"Well —" I started.

But Granny Deaver instantly interrupted me. "I'm a ghost. I'm supposed to howl. How dare you complain about it?" She turned to my parents. "Young people have no respect. No respect."

Before anyone could reply, Granny Deaver turned her attention to Jeff. "Sit up straight, young man. Do you want curved bones like mine? Would you like to be a ghost like me, walking all hunched over? Sit up straight!"

"I don't *believe* this," Jeff whispered to me, rolling his eyes. "She's dead — and she's still picking on me!"

I turned to Mom and Dad. Mom shrugged helplessly. Dad just shook his head.

We couldn't talk. We couldn't make a plan about how to get rid of Granny Deaver. Not while she was sitting right there, grumbling and complaining. And listening to every word we said.

"Uh . . . we have a lot to do today," Mom started. "We have to get everything ready for Kelly's party."

"Party?" Granny Deaver snapped. "Party? How can you have a party when I just *died*?"

"It's my birthday!" I cried. "We've been planning this party for weeks."

Granny Deaver rose up from the table. Her skin, her clothes, her eyes — had all faded to a pale green. "Seems like a strange time to have a party," she said, her nose in the air. "Am I invited? I really don't think I'm in a party mood."

"Huh? Invited?" I gasped.

And then I totally lost it.

"No! You're *not* invited!" I screamed. "I don't care if you're in the mood or not! You're not

27

invited! It's my twelfth birthday party, and all my friends are coming. And I don't want you to spoil it!"

I was breathing hard when I finished that speech, glaring sharply at Granny Deaver, hands on my waist.

Her mouth opened to reply. But then she closed it. She rose up over the kitchen, growing paler, so pale she was difficult to see. As if her body was made of a wisp of smoke.

"I can take a hint," she said finally, in a whisper. Her eyes grew dull and blank. She faded toward the door. "I can take a hint. I know when I'm not wanted."

She floated from the room.

All four of us stood in silence, staring at the doorway.

"She got so pale," Jeff said finally. "So weak. Do you think she disappeared forever?"

"No," Dad replied, shaking his head. "I saw her float up the stairs. She probably went to her room."

"And will she stay up there?" I asked. "Will she stay up in the attic, and not come down and terrify my friends?"

Mom shrugged again. "We'll see," she said softly. "We'll see."

*   *   *

We worked all morning getting the house ready. Jeff helped me with decorations. Then he went with Dad to the bakery to get the cake. Mom baked homemade pizzas and made a big salad.

A little after two o'clock, the doorbell rang. My first party guest.

I pulled open the front door and greeted my friend Gina Lang.

"Happy Birthday, Kelly," she said.

Then she stepped into the house — raised her hands to her face — and screamed.

6

Huh? Gina — what's wrong?" I demanded.

I spun to the steps. Had Granny Deaver appeared?

No. No sign of her.

"I forgot your present!" Gina exclaimed. "Oh! I don't believe it! I'll be right back!"

She turned and ran back out the front door. Through the window, I could see her running across the street to her house.

I let out a long sigh of relief.

Granny Deaver, please stay up in your room, I prayed silently, crossing my fingers on both hands. *Please don't spoil my party.*

A short while later, everyone had arrived. We all talked and hung out for a while.

"Sorry to hear about your grandmother,"

my friend Wendy Martin said as I made my way to the couch to open presents.

"She wasn't really my grandmother," I replied.

I raised my eyes to the stairs. No sign of Granny Deaver.

"But she lived with you for a long time — right?" Wendy asked.

I nodded. "Yes. A long, long time."

I started opening presents. Gina gave me three CDs I really wanted. My friend Nedra gave me two tickets to a rock concert downtown — one for me and one for her.

I was having a pretty good time. We were all laughing and kidding around. I got some totally cool presents.

I wanted to enjoy every minute of the party. I mean, a person only turns twelve once.

But I couldn't be totally comfortable. I couldn't really be relaxed — because I kept watching the stairway, watching for Granny Deaver to appear.

After I opened my presents, we hung out for a while longer. Then Mom brought out the home-baked pizzas, and we moved into the dining room to eat.

The party was going really well. And it was helping to cheer me up a lot.

For some reason, in the middle of lunch, we all started singing camp songs. Wendy, Gina, and I had spent last summer at the same sleepaway camp. And we remembered every word of every song.

We were singing and laughing at the same time. Then Nedra took two pepperonis off her pizza and put them over her eyes. She looked like some kind of red-eyed monster.

It wasn't that funny, but it cracked us up. And a few seconds later, we *all* had pepperoni eyes.

"Okay, okay. Calm down, everyone," Mom called from the kitchen. "It's cake time."

Dad hurried to get his camera.

"Here we go!" Mom declared. She stepped into the dining room carrying the cake on a big platter, the pink and yellow candles glowing. "Ready to sing?" she asked.

Before anyone could start, I heard a low moan.

Wendy let out a startled cry. A few other girls cried out.

I turned to the doorway.

Granny Deaver billowed into the room. She smiled a toothless smile. One of her eyeballs had fallen out. She squinted with an empty eye socket.

"Kelly!" she rasped. "Will you save a slice of cake for your dear, dead granny?"

7

The disgusting green ghost floated over the dining room table.

Everyone screamed.

Chairs scraped, then toppled over as girls scrambled to stand up.

Mom dropped the cake.

The platter cracked, and the cake made a sick *SPLAAT* sound as it hit the floor.

Squinting with her one eye, Granny Deaver tossed her head back and cackled.

"Afraid of a dead person?" she shrieked. "What's wrong with you girls? Afraid of a dead person?"

Screaming shrilly, my friends scrambled to the front door.

Cokes spilled. Another chair fell to the floor.

33

Nedra tripped and fell. With a frightened cry, she jumped to her feet and ran to catch up to the others.

"Wait —!" I shrieked. "Don't go! Wait —!"

But they were out of the house in seconds. Wendy was the last to leave. She turned back. She stared up at the cackling ghost over the dining room table — let out another scream — and vanished out the door.

"No — please —!" I called after them weakly. "Please, don't go —!"

Gone. They were all gone.

I turned to Granny Deaver, my hands tightening into fists. "How could you *do* this to me?" I shrieked. "How could you ruin my birthday party like that?"

Dad set down his camera and hurried over to me. He put a hand on my trembling shoulder.

"Aren't you going to take my picture?" Granny Deaver demanded. She grinned, and a tooth fell from her mouth. It landed in the birthday cake, which lay in a heap on the dining room carpet.

"How could you do this?" I shouted again. I took deep breaths to keep from crying.

Granny Deaver slowly floated down to the floor. Her hair was wild around her face. I saw to my horror that her chin had cracked open. I could see bone underneath the skin.

She bent down and lifted a chunk of birthday cake off the floor. "Chocolate?" She turned to me and made a disgusted face. "Who gets chocolate for a birthday cake? You know I don't like chocolate. What's wrong with vanilla?"

"It's not your birthday!" I shrieked at the top of my lungs. *"It's my birthday — and you ruined it!"*

She gasped, as if stung. "Have a little respect for the dead, Kelly," she scolded.

She took a small bite of the cake. "I can't taste a thing," she told us. "Not a thing. I guess the dead can't taste."

She sighed. "But if I could taste it, I'm sure it'd be way too rich. Next time, get a normal cake. Get vanilla. Or even a nice lemon cake."

That was it. I couldn't take any more.

I let out a furious cry. I broke away from my dad — and rushed at the old ghost with both fists raised.

I don't know what I thought I was doing. Actually, I wasn't thinking at all. I was in too big a rage to think.

"Go away!" I shrieked at the old ghost. "Go away! Go away! Go awaaaay!"

To my surprise, Granny Deaver coiled back. Her one eye grew wide. She raised both hands and arched her back, like an animal about to attack.

She bared her few remaining teeth and let out a shrill, animal hiss.

Her eye glowed bright red. Her whole body billowed up like smoke from a chimney. And her face began to change.

Her features shrank as her head grew. Long fangs slid over her broken chin.

Claws curled out from her bony, raised hands.

She hissed at me again, an ugly, menacing hiss.

Her putrid, cold breath swept over me.

"Kelly . . . ," she rasped through her fangs. "Kelly . . . be careful. I'm a ghost, Kelly. I'm dead. I have my *evil* side now. You don't really want to see my evil side — *do* you?"

8

angs bared, claws outstretched, she rose above me, ready to attack.

With a startled cry, I shrank back. And lowered my fists.

Another animal hiss escaped her lips. Her red eye flashed.

I stared in horror at the ugly, hissing creature. This isn't Granny Deaver, I told myself. This is some kind of creature . . . some kind of dead creature using her face, her shape.

"Be careful, Kelly!" she rasped again. And swiped a claw close to my face. "Be careful. Or I —"

She stopped suddenly.

Her mouth dropped open. The strange, animal face twisted in surprise.

The claws slid back into her hands. The

fangs vanished, and her head began to reshape as Granny Deaver's head.

The old ghost had a startled expression on her face. As if she couldn't control what was happening to her.

"I'm . . . tired," she whispered. "So tired."

She turned away from us slowly. She faded, almost to nothing. Then shimmered back, faint and dim.

Floating low over the floor, she wearily made her way to the stairs. As she started up, she let out sigh after sigh, as if each step was a struggle for her.

I huddled close to Dad and watched until she vanished up the stairs. Then I rested my head on his shoulder, shutting my eyes.

"Wow," I heard Jeff mutter. And then he repeated it. "Wow."

"What a mess," Mom said softly. "I'll never get the chocolate stains off the carpet."

Dad uttered an unhappy sigh. "We've got a bigger problem than chocolate stains," he said.

"Yeah," I agreed. "We have a disgusting, frightening ghost in the house." A chill ran down my back.

"She looked pretty weak before she left," Jeff murmured. "Maybe she's going to fade away."

"She was weak at breakfast," I recalled. "Then she came back stronger than ever." I sighed. "She's probably up in her room, resting up. Getting ready to spoil our lives in some new way."

Mom shuddered. "I . . . I'm really frightened now," she confessed. She took Dad's hand and held on to it. "What are we going to do?"

Dad gazed back at her for the longest time without replying. Finally he said, "We have to ask her to leave."

"That won't do any good!" I cried. "She won't just leave. Why should she?"

"Where would she go?" Mom asked Dad.

"Back to the graveyard, where she belongs!" Dad replied.

"She won't," I repeated glumly. "She won't go. I know she won't. She's going to stay here with us forever."

Dad shook his head. "There's *got* to be a way to get rid of her. But how? How do you get rid of a ghost?"

That night, we went out for dinner. We didn't want to take a chance on Granny Deaver spoiling another meal.

We ate our food without talking.

What was there to say?

"This was the worst birthday of my life," I grumbled as we finished our dessert.

"At least it's a birthday you'll never forget!" Dad replied, forcing a smile.

I knew he was trying to cheer me up. But I didn't want to be cheered up.

"Could we stay at a motel or something tonight?" Jeff asked. "I really don't want to go home."

"I know what we can do!" I cried. "We can sell the house and move!"

"What good will that do?" Mom asked.

"We won't tell Granny Deaver our new address," I explained.

"You mean sell someone the house with a ghost living in it?" Dad asked. "That wouldn't be a very nice thing to do — would it?"

"Who cares?" I moaned.

"Maybe she'll be gone when we get back," Mom said. She held up both hands. She had her fingers crossed. "Maybe Granny Deaver realized she was making us unhappy, and she went back to the cemetery."

"Yeah. Maybe," I said softly. But I didn't believe it. None of us did.

Later, I was lying on my back in bed, trying to fall asleep, when I heard Granny Deaver begin to howl.

I gazed up toward the attic as the sound of the howls floated down over me. Soft at first. Almost a whisper. Then shrill and loud as an ambulance siren.

Animal howls. Like a wolf baying at the moon.

Howl after howl.

I pressed my hands against my ears. But I couldn't shut out the frightening sounds.

I tried covering my head with my pillow. But that didn't help, either.

And then I heard the doorbell ring downstairs. Followed by several hard raps on the door.

I jumped from bed, the howls still ringing in my ears. I ran downstairs.

I was first to reach the door.

"Who — who's there?" I stammered.

"Open up, please." A man's voice, loud and firm. "It's the police."

9

"Huh?" I let out a startled gasp and pulled open the door.

Mom, Dad, and Jeff appeared behind me.

We stared out at a young officer with curly blond hair, round cheeks, and flashing blue eyes. He didn't look like a policeman. He looked about eighteen!

He held his uniform cap in one hand and a police badge in the other.

"Can we help you?" Dad asked, pulling his bathrobe belt tight.

Mom brushed back her hair with both hands. "Is there a problem, officer?"

The young cop nodded. "We've received complaints from your neighbors. About loud howls coming from your house."

"Uh . . . it's just our dog," Dad told him. "We're very sorry. We'll get him quiet."

"No, it isn't!" I cried. "We don't own a dog!"

Dad shouldn't make up a story. Maybe the police officer can help us, I thought. Maybe he can help us get rid of Granny Deaver.

The officer slipped his badge into his back pocket and narrowed his eyes at me. "It isn't your dog howling?"

"Kelly — please!" Dad pleaded.

I ignored him. "It's a ghost," I told the officer. "We have a ghost in our attic. And she's driving us crazy."

A smile spread over the cop's smooth, round face. "Yeah. For sure!" he said, snickering. "A ghost. I'll believe it when I see it."

But then, his smile faded. And his blue eyes bulged as he stared into our house.

We all turned to see what he was staring at.

Granny Deaver! She roared into the living room. Shimmering, bright green. Floating over the furniture. Her fangs sliding out of her mouth. Raising her curled claws.

And roaring. Roaring a lion's roar.

"Nooooooo!" The officer opened his mouth in a cry of disbelief. His cap fell to the ground. But he didn't stop to pick it up.

43

He turned and bolted off the front stoop.

"Hey, wait!" I called. "Please?"

But he never looked back. He ran to his cruiser in the driveway. Jumped in. And backed down the drive without even closing the door. Backed down and squealed away.

The ghost roared and screeched behind us.

I turned and gasped, horrified by its snarling creature face, so evil . . . so dead.

"Did you try to turn your old granny over to the police?" it growled, rising higher, closer.

"N-no —" I started.

"LIAR!" the ghost screeched.

And then it swept over me. Raised both hands — and swiped its long, sharp claws across my face.

10

"hhhh." A weak cry escaped my throat.

I stumbled back. Waited for the pain to rush over me.

Waited . . .

And then laughed. A high, startled laugh.

Because I couldn't feel a thing.

I rubbed my face. No scratches. Nothing.

The old ghost roared and swiped its claws over me again.

I stood there without flinching. "You can't hurt me!" I cried. "I can't feel a thing! You're helpless!"

"Noooooo!" It was the ghost's turn to wail. It opened its jaws in a long, loud howl of protest.

And then it exploded. Exploded into a million, tiny green pieces. The pieces floated in the air for a few seconds, like confetti falling down.

And then they vanished.

And the four of us were alone in the living room. All alone. Without a ghost. Staring at each other in shocked silence.

Jeff was the first to speak. "Kelly — how did you do that?" he asked.

"I stood up to it," I replied. "Remember when Granny Deaver's ghost got weak at breakfast? And later, after my party? Both times I got angry and stood up to her. And both times she became weak and frail. I guess a ghost can't exist if you stand up to it."

"And now she's gone!" Mom cried happily. "And we can all return to normal!"

We were so happy. We hugged each other. We cried. Then we couldn't stop laughing. Such a wonderful, joyful moment.

We were still laughing when we heard the knock on the front door.

"Who can that be?" Mom asked. She pulled open the door.

And we stared out at a horrifying group of people. Men and women, all bent and twisted. Their eyes sunken and as blank as glass. Their faces dead.

Dead . . . dead people. Green and rotting.

46

At least a dozen of them. Limping up the lawn. Climbing onto the front stoop.

"Who — who are you?" I choked out.

"We're from the cemetery," a hunched man whispered, staring up at us with vacant eye sockets. "We met Granny Deaver there. She was so nice. She invited us to come stay."

"Huh?" I gasped. "Granny Deaver —? She — *what*?"

They crawled and hobbled past us. Into the house.

"Where is Granny Deaver?" the hunched man asked.

"She . . . she isn't here," Dad told them.

The dead man sank into the couch and put his feet up. "That's okay," he said. "We'll wait."

Spin the Wheel
of Horror

Introduction

SLIM: Are you feeling lucky today?

LEFTY: Yeah. A lucky thing happened to me. I found a cute little puppy on the street.

RIGHTY: Wow. That *is* lucky.

LEFTY: I know. It was *delicious.*

RIGHTY: I've got my lucky rabbit's foot right here.

SLIM: But it's still attached to the rabbit.

RIGHTY: No *wonder* it won't fit in my pocket!

SLIM: Well, if you're feeling lucky, maybe you'd like to try playing a game.

RIGHTY: Know what my favorite game is?

LEFTY: What?

RIGHTY: *Spin the Human.*

SLIM: That's not the game I was thinking

of. I meant the TV game show in our next story — *Spin the Wheel of Horror.* A boy named Tyler and his family find the show *very* exciting. They have only one small problem. They can't tell where the GAME ends and the HORROR begins. . . .

1

I stared out the back window of our car and shivered with excitement.

I still couldn't believe it. Mom, Dad, Emmy and I — Tyler Banks, age twelve — were actually going to be contestants on *The Wheel of Horror,* the coolest game show on TV.

The way the show works is this: The audience and the host dress up like monsters. The contestants spin a big wheel, and they have to go wherever it lands. It's always a scary place, like the Monster Maze or Ghoul Garage. Of course, nothing on the show is real. But the special effects are great.

The object of the game is not to scream. You can whimper. You can gasp. You can moan and groan. But if you scream, you lose.

If you make it all the way through without

screaming, you win. And I mean BIG. Like, one hundred thousand dollars!

"This is going to be so cool!" I exclaimed as Dad drove along the winding road. I turned to my sister. "Emmy, remember last week's show? When the mummy chased a whole family through the audience?"

"Yeah, that was awesome! And I liked when the other family went through the Haunted House and ghosts popped out everywhere." Emmy snickered. "I couldn't believe it — those people screamed before they even got to the second floor!"

I laughed, but inside I felt a little nervous. I hoped we didn't get stuck in the Haunted House. Not only did it have ghosts, it had bats. Bats are not exactly my favorite creatures — even fake ones.

"Has anyone seen a Biggie Burger sign?" Dad asked.

"We're not stopping, are we?" Emmy cried. "I don't want to be late for the show."

"No, we're not going to stop," Dad assured us. "We'll have a feast later, if we win." He peered anxiously out the windshield. "But I should have seen that sign by now. It's in the directions."

"All I see are trees," I said. "All I've seen for miles are trees."

Mom glanced nervously at Dad. "Are you going the right way?"

"I'm not sure," he admitted. "Tyler is right — there's nothing but forest for miles. I may have missed the turnoff."

I checked my watch. We had only fifteen minutes to get there.

"Maybe you should turn around," Mom suggested.

"Right," I agreed quickly.

Dad shook his head. "Let's go a little farther."

"Hurry, Dad!" Emmy cried. "Please! We don't want to make everybody wait!"

"We won't," Dad said. He pushed down on the gas pedal.

I mashed my face against the window as the car sped down the road. All I saw was forest. No Biggie Burger sign. No TV studio sign. Just thick, dark forest.

"Faster!" Emmy cried. "Faster!"

"Emmy, I can't go any faster or . . ." Dad suddenly stopped talking.

That's when we heard the wail of a siren.

I twisted around to look out the back window. A green and white police car roared toward us. Its lights flashed, and its siren rose and fell shrilly.

"Oh, man!" I groaned. "Now we'll be late for sure!"

Dad pulled to the side of the road and stopped. The police car screeched to a halt a few yards behind us. I watched as the policeman climbed out and walked toward us.

"We're in major trouble," I muttered. "Now we'll never make it to the TV studio in time."

The policeman marched up and rapped on the driver's window. Dad rolled it down. The policeman shoved his hat back and leaned in.

I turned to the front — and let out a terrified scream.

It wasn't a policeman at all. It was the most hideous monster I had ever seen.

2

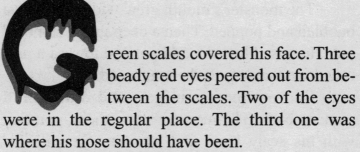reen scales covered his face. Three beady red eyes peered out from between the scales. Two of the eyes were in the regular place. The third one was where his nose should have been.

Instead of lips, he had a small black hole that made a bubbling, whistling noise as he breathed through it.

Mom hunched up against the passenger door. "Step on it, John!" she whispered. "Hurry!"

"Let's get out of here!" I urged in a shaky voice.

But Dad just threw back his head and laughed. "It's a good thing we're not on the TV show yet. We'd lose for sure!"

"Huh?" I stared at the monster. His mouth bubbled, and the scales flapped. His three eyes spun around like marbles. "You think he's part of the show?"

"Of course he is." Dad laughed again. "We must have come in by another entrance, and he's here to guide us. We're in the right place, after all."

Dad smiled up at the monster. "We were afraid we'd be late. Where is the studio? Can you show us where to park?"

The monster's mouth grew wide. The saliva bubbled and popped. Then a deep growl rumbled out. He raised his arm and pointed toward a narrow drive that led off the main road.

Dad put the car in gear and drove off. I glanced back. The monster stood there, pointing with his scaly hand and watching us with his three spinning eyes.

"Great costume," I murmured. "But why didn't he say anything?"

"That's part of the fun," Dad said. He glanced into the rearview mirror. "Better get your screaming done now, kids. We're almost there."

In another minute, we pulled into a parking lot next to an old brick building. "Are you sure this is the TV studio?" Mom asked doubtfully. "It looks so run-down."

Mom was right. The building looked like an abandoned factory. Dirty red bricks. A sagging roof. A warped wooden sign hung next to the front door, but the letters on it were too faded to read.

"This place creeps me out," Emmy declared.

"This is probably the back entrance," Dad told her.

"Right," I agreed as we climbed out of the car. "The guide pointed us here, didn't he?" I couldn't wait to get inside and be on the show. "Come on, let's hurry!"

The big door creaked loudly when Dad pulled it open. He hurried us into the building. The door slammed shut with a bang.

I glanced around. At least, I *tried* to glance around. But I couldn't see a thing.

The place was totally dark.

"John, I really think we're in the wrong place," Mom whispered nervously. "It feels completely empty."

"It can't be," Dad insisted. "All we have to do is walk a little way and we'll find the show."

I took a shuffling step through the dark. Then another.

And something grabbed me around the waist.

3

"**D**ad!" I shouted.

The lights burst on.

Mom and Dad and Emmy gasped. I froze.

A tall, huge, skinny creature had me in its grip.

Gray-white bones jutted through its papery skin. Dark eyes peered at me from deep, bony eye sockets. Its yellow teeth made clicking noises inside its shiny skull.

The creature gave me a hard push toward Mom, Dad, and Emmy. Croaking like a sick frog, it waved long, bony arms. We stepped back. The creature made a shooing motion with its arms.

We turned and ran down a long hallway. The skeleton creature chased after us.

Around a corner. Down another hall. Through a set of double doors.

We staggered to a stop in front of blinding, bright lights.

"Let's hear a big hand for today's contestants on *The Wheel of Horror*!" a voice boomed. "Let's hear it for the Banks family!"

Loud applause burst out. I peered out through the lights and saw werewolves, ghosts, mummies, alien buglike creatures — all clapping and grinning at us. The skeleton who'd chased us to the stage stood off to the side, jumping up and down and clapping its bony hands together.

"What did I tell you?" Dad shouted over the noise. "This is the place, all right!"

The clapping suddenly grew louder. A tall man wearing a dark suit and a swirling black cape strode toward us into the spotlight.

Did I say *man*?

Make that *wolf*man.

Emmy nudged me. "Tyler, is that a great costume or what?"

I nodded. Bristly brown fur covered his hands and head and face. His eyes were dark and piercing. Even up close, they looked like an animal's.

"Welcome, everyone!" he rumbled in a

deep voice. His long white teeth dripped with saliva. "Welcome!"

"We're really excited to be here!" Dad shouted over the applause.

"We've waited a long time for this," Mom added.

"So you're ready to begin, are you?" the emcee asked.

"We can't wait!" I told him. Now that I knew we were actually at the show, I felt really excited. "And we're not going to scream," I declared. "No way!"

The audience cheered.

"Let's get started," the emcee said. "First, I have one question for you."

He leaned close to us. His dark eyes gleamed with excitement. "Would you like to be baked?" he asked. "Or fried?"

4

Huh? I'd seen this show plenty of times. The host never asked that question before.

"Baked or fried?" he repeated. "Pick one."

"Pick one! Pick one!" the audience chanted.

I turned to Mom and Dad. "What's going on?" I asked. "This isn't part of the show."

"It's just a joke," Dad insisted.

"Baked or fried?" the audience chanted. "Pick one! Pick one!"

Dad gathered us in a circle. "Let's decide. Honey, what do you choose?"

"Tell him baked," Mom finally said. "It's much healthier than fried."

"Time's up!" the emcee cried. "What is your decision?"

"We pick baked," Dad announced.

The audience roared. "Excellent choice!" the wolfman host declared. "And now, let's spin the wheel."

The emcee waved his arm. A tall woman with black hair, red lips, and gleaming sharp teeth pulled a huge wheel onstage. The wheel was divided into sections, like a pie. Each section had the name of a place written on it — the Haunted House, Slay Land, the Hotel for Ghouls, the Tunnel of Terror, Monster Mall, and Gross National Park.

The tall woman waved us toward the wheel. We all took hold of the big handle and pulled down hard.

The audience clapped as the wheel spun around and around. Fast at first, then slower and slower.

The pointer hovered over the Haunted House. I crossed my fingers that it wouldn't stop. Then the wheel inched around a little more, to Slay Land.

Finally, the wheel stopped.

"The Hotel for Ghouls!" the host announced. "All right — here we go!" He waved his arm toward the back of the stage.

A curtain rose, revealing a hotel lobby.

An old, deserted hotel lobby.

Cobwebs hung from the ceiling and draped across the front desk. Dead plants stood in grimy pots.

The wall had rows of small cubbyholes — mailboxes for the guests. Greenish-brown slime oozed from one of them. The rug was torn and stained. The elevator doors were cracked and rusted.

Here we go! I thought. All we have to do is keep our mouths shut, and we'll win the game!

"Check into the Hotel for Ghouls," the host declared. "We hope you check out!"

He turned and strode away. Then a wall came up between us and the audience.

Everything grew silent.

"Hello?" Dad called out. "Anybody here?"

No answer.

We crept forward. The floorboards creaked. Something is going to happen, I told myself. Something really scary. Get ready for it, Tyler, and don't scream.

"Hello?" Dad called again.

A little silver bell sat on the desk. On top of it was a skeleton hand. The bony forefinger rested on the bell.

Oh, man, a stupid plastic hand, I thought. That definitely won't make me scream.

I shoved the hand away and banged on the bell. A puff of dust rose up. A black spider scurried over the desk and disappeared into a crack.

Nobody appeared.

"Ring it again," Emmy murmured.

I reached toward the bell. And froze.

Something wrapped itself around my leg. Under my jeans, right above my ankle. Something smooth and dry.

And alive.

I could feel it wriggling slowly upward. Climbing my leg.

I jumped back, my heart pounding in terror, and opened my mouth to scream.

5

Emmy clamped her hand over my mouth. "What's wrong with you?" she whispered. "You can't scream yet! The game just started!"

I yanked her hand away. "There's something on my leg!"

"Stop trying to scare . . ." Emmy stopped. Her eyes grew wide. "Me too!" she cried. "Something's on me too!"

I gulped. Then I carefully reached down and stuck my hand under the cuff of my jeans.

I whipped my hand out and gasped. A long, skinny, black snake wriggled through my fingers.

Keep cool, I told myself. It's rubber, that's all. Don't scream. It's all part of the game.

Emmy let out a squeak. I turned to her. She held a snake too.

I grabbed hers — and flung them both away.

Then I took a deep breath. The floor — it appeared to move! "Ohh." I let out a roar as I saw dozens of snakes writhing across the floor. Hundreds! Hundreds of wriggling, hissing, twisting snakes!

Emmy let out another squeak.

I bit my lip to keep from screaming.

We both backed away and bumped against the desk. As I turned to pull myself up, I saw Mom and Dad. They stood against one of the lobby walls, mouths open in horror as snakes twisted around their ankles.

Before I could move, another snake began to slither up my leg. This one was bigger than the others — long and fat, with orange speckles and beady black eyes. It squirmed quickly up my leg and coiled itself around my left shoulder.

"Tyler!" Emmy shouted. "They're pulling me down!"

"Me too!" I choked out.

Snakes covered my legs like tight rubber bands, pulling and tugging. My knees buckled.

I grabbed hold of the desk to keep from being dragged down. Then another fat snake crawled up, wrapped around my right arm, and began to pull hard.

My fingers started slipping off the edge of the desk. I began to sag. My knees touched the floor.

A snake slithered up my back and began to coil around my neck. Its dry skin rasped against my throat. Its tongue flickered in and out. Cold black eyes stared into mine as it bared its sharp fangs at my face.

Snakes swarmed up my arms and across my back. They wrapped themselves around me and began to squeeze, tighter and tighter.

My whole family was covered in a sea of tangled, hissing snakes.

I can't hang on! I thought. I'm falling! I'll be buried alive!

6

swayed back and forth with dizziness. My eyes bulged.

Everything grew fuzzy and dark.

I couldn't breathe!

A scream of terror was building inside me. Way down in my chest. Forcing its way up my throat.

Don't do it! I told myself. They want you to scream. If you scream, you lose. Don't give in!

Get on top of the desk! I instructed myself. Then maybe you can pull them off.

Gasping for air, I reached up and grabbed hold of the snake that twisted around my neck. It writhed and hissed at me in fury. Its tongue flicked against my palm.

I gritted my teeth and yanked as hard as I could. The snake whipped back and forth, hunching its thick body and trying to fling itself out of my grip.

I held on tight and tugged again. The snake kept fighting, but I finally unwound it from around my neck — and flung it away.

"Ahh!" I sucked in a deep breath of air. Then I grabbed hold of the desk and dragged myself onto the top. I yanked a snake off my wrist and tossed it to the floor. Then I started peeling them from around my legs and arms.

"Tyler!" Emmy called out. "Help me!"

I turned to her. A snake had wound itself around Emmy's head like a bandana.

I reached down, grabbed Emmy's hand, and pulled her up onto the desk. The snake whipped its head around and glared at me. I grabbed it behind the eyes, yanked it loose, and threw it onto the floor.

As Emmy and I began unwinding the snakes from our legs, we both tried not to scream. Emmy made little squeaking sounds. I clenched my teeth.

Finally, we got all the snakes loose.

For a moment, the snakes swarmed around the desk, trying to climb up. But finally, they slithered away.

"Do you think they're gone for good?" Emmy asked breathlessly.

I shrugged. "I don't know. I hope so."

"Were they real?" Emmy asked. "They felt so real."

"I don't know," I admitted. "They couldn't be real. It's only a TV show — right?"

I turned to Mom and Dad. "Are you okay?" I asked. "Mom? Dad?"

They were gone.

7

"**W**here *are* they?" Emmy cried. "The last time I saw them, they were surrounded by snakes. But the snakes are gone, and Mom and Dad wouldn't just wander away and leave us!"

"Come on, let's look around," I said. "They've got to be here somewhere."

Emmy and I hopped down from the desk and began to search the lobby. As I walked across the dusty rug, something brushed against my face.

I gasped.

"What?" Emmy cried. "What is it?"

I held my breath and reached my hands up to something soft and sticky clinging to my skin. "A cobweb," I muttered. "Just a cobweb."

I peeled the cobweb off and wiped my fingers on my jeans. At least there wasn't a spider in it.

"Mom? Dad?" Emmy called softly. "Tyler, where are they?"

"Ssh!" I held my finger to my lips. "I heard something!"

We both stood still, listening. In the distance, we heard a low hum. A motor.

"The elevator!" I cried. "Come on. Maybe Mom and Dad are on it!"

We rushed over to the elevator and waited. We heard a grinding, thumping sound. Then it stopped.

The elevator doors creaked and groaned. And slowly slid open.

Inside stood the elevator operator. Alone. He wore a red uniform with gold buttons. A red cap with a black brim that threw a shadow across his face. "Can I take you to your room?" he croaked.

I started to get in. But Emmy grabbed my arm. "Is the game almost over?" she asked the elevator operator.

The guy shook his head. "Get in. The game is just beginning."

Big deal, I thought. We made it through the snakes, didn't we? Anything else will be a piece of cake.

"Get in," the guy repeated. "Room thirteen."

"Are our parents up in the room?" I asked.

"Maybe," he rumbled. "Get in and you'll see."

The guy's voice gave me the creeps, but I knew it was just part of the show. No way would I scream over that.

We stepped into the elevator. The doors creaked shut. The humming noise started. As the car began to rise, the operator turned to us.

I gasped. So did Emmy.

One side of the guy's face was normal. A dark eyebrow. A blue eye. Mustache. Grinning mouth.

But the other half was a total mess. The eyeball hung out of its socket, oozing thick yellow slime. A scar ran through the eyebrow and down to the lips. Half the teeth were cracked and covered with green fuzz.

"Maybe we'll just get off on the second floor and take the stairs the rest of the way up," I choked out.

The guy took a step toward us.

Emmy and I pressed against the back wall.

The guy took another step. I felt like screaming. But I kept my mouth shut and swallowed hard.

The guy came closer.

And the light went out.

Emmy squeaked.

I clenched my teeth.

Then I slid along the wall, trying to keep away from the elevator operator.

Where was he? I couldn't see a thing!

"Emmy?" I called out.

No answer.

"Emmy, are you there?" Fingers brushed my shoulder. I jumped. "Emmy?" I yelled.

"Here I am," she replied, grabbing my hand. "But the elevator guy —"

The light suddenly burst back on.

The guy had disappeared.

"Whoa! Where did he go?" Emmy asked. "How could he just vanish like that?"

I didn't have a chance to reply.

The elevator jerked hard.

And began to fall.

8

The elevator plunged down fast.

I bit my lip. Don't scream, I told myself.

It's just a TV show. It's just a game.

Don't scream.

I grabbed hold of the railing and tried to brace myself. Emmy squeezed her eyes shut. My stomach flipped over. And over.

The elevator plunged down for another few seconds. Then it bounced. Hard.

Emmy and I fell to the floor. The car bounced up. Then down. Up again. Finally, it stopped with a loud thud.

"You okay?" I asked.

She nodded. "Let's just get out of this thing."

As I reached for the button, the doors creaked open. Emmy and I rushed out.

We found ourselves in a gray basement room. Thick, greenish-black scum covered the tiled walls and floor. Rusty beach chairs stood around an enormous swimming pool.

"What's that disgusting smell?" Emmy cried.

I pointed to the pool. It was filled with moldy green gunk that bubbled and swirled and made little spitting sounds. Wisps of steam rose up. The air smelled like rotten eggs.

I breathed through my mouth, but it didn't help. The smell made my stomach turn.

"Sick," Emmy choked out. "Let's go."

We turned back to the elevator. The doors had closed. Greenish-black slime covered the button. But I forced myself to push it.

The doors didn't open.

"Let's start walking," Emmy said. "Maybe we can find the lobby again."

"Good idea." We began to edge our way along the pool. Inches from the slimy stuff that squished and oozed.

"It's so dark in here," Emmy complained, walking ahead of me. "I can't see a . . . whoa!"

Emmy slipped on the tiles and fell on her

side. Then she began rolling. Rolling over the slimy tiles, straight for the pool.

I skidded across the floor and grabbed her arm just before she rolled into the bubbling green gunk. We slipped and slid, trying to get to our feet.

As we finally scrambled up, we heard something at the other end of the room.

Echoing off the tiled walls.

Footsteps.

"Tyler," Emmy whispered. "We're not alone."

9

The footsteps grew louder.

Here we go again, I thought. Will it be scarier than the snakes or the falling elevator?

I didn't want to wait around to find out.

"Tyler, let's go!" Emmy whispered. She grabbed hold of my arm and tried to help me move.

We both slipped and slid. And fell again.

The echoing footsteps grew louder.

Closer.

"Forget walking!" I whispered to Emmy.

On our hands and knees, we began to crawl across the floor. The greenish-black slime soaked through my jeans and oozed up between my fingers. It felt like mud, but it smelled like rotting garbage.

I could hear the footsteps better now. Louder. Closer.

Just a game, I reminded myself. It's just a game.

"Emmy? Tyler?" a voice suddenly called out.

Dad's voice.

I slithered to a stop and turned around. Through the green haze, I saw Mom and Dad making their way across the tiles.

"Over here!" I called.

"Thank goodness!" Mom cried. She held Dad's hand to keep from falling as they hurried over to us. "Are you two all right?"

"I guess." Emmy and I carefully rose to our feet and tried to rub some of the slime from our clothes. "What happened to you?" I asked. "How did we get separated?"

"Good question," Dad replied. "One minute we were battling those snakes. And the next thing I knew, a secret panel opened in the lobby wall right behind us. We couldn't get back to you. We've been wandering around, searching for you ever since."

"Never mind that," Mom told him. "I don't like this one bit. Is this *The Wheel of Horror* or not?"

"Of course it is," Dad insisted. "Just smell

that pool. And look at Emmy and Tyler. They're covered with slime. If that isn't *horrible,* what is?"

"I still think we're in the wrong place," Mom argued. "The game isn't anything like this! Where's the audience? Where is the host? We're all alone in here!"

I held up both hands. "Stop arguing. Please. We have to find a way out of here — before I throw up."

"Let's try to find some stairs," Emmy suggested. "The elevator doors won't open."

But just then, the elevator doors *did* open.

And out stepped two hideous creatures.

Huge creatures, taller than Dad! Thick fur covered their arms and legs, but their feet and hands were red and glistening, like big pieces of raw meat. Their heads were the size of basketballs, with leathery lips and burning red eyes.

"Look at those teeth!" Mom whispered. "I think they're real! I don't think this is a game show at all!"

With a wild snarl, the ghouls charged toward us.

We turned and ran.

The ghouls raced after us, bellowing in rage.

We raced along the side of the pool and

skidded around the corner. "I'm slipping!" Emmy cried. I grabbed one of her hands. Dad grabbed the other. Emmy caught her balance, and we all kept running.

The ghouls kept running too, their huge feet slapping through the slime.

Holding hands, we raced along the short end of the pool. But as we turned another corner, the floor suddenly began to tilt.

We crashed to our knees. The floor tilted some more. We began to slide toward the pool.

"Tyler!" Emmy called out. "Catch me!"

I reached for her, but she was too far away. I tried to grab on to the tiles, but my fingers slipped on the green scum.

The floor tilted higher. Emmy rolled past me. I heard a loud splash.

Then Dad and Mom rolled by.

Two more splashes.

I tried to hang on, but I couldn't. The floor tilted straight up. I slid down until I fell into the bubbling, steaming green goo.

10

wanted to scream, but I couldn't.

I barely had time to take a breath before the thick green ooze closed over my head.

I felt myself sinking. I stuck my arms out to grab hold of something or someone. But all I felt was thick, squishy slime.

My feet hit the bottom of the pool. I bent my knees and started to push up.

But then the pool floor tilted. And I was sliding down again. Until I tumbled to a sudden stop.

Whistles and applause and loud cheering broke out all around me.

Huh? Where were we? What had happened?

I shook my head and took a deep breath. I wiped the slime from my eyes and nose and gazed around.

Mom, Dad, and Emmy huddled next to me, pulling green gunk out of their hair.

In front of us sat the audience of monsters, clapping and cheering.

"I can't believe it!" I cried, pointing out to the audience. "We're back on the stage!"

"Indeed you are!" the host agreed. He strode up in his swirling black cape and smiled at us. "Congratulations!"

I climbed to my feet. "You mean it's over?" I asked. "We win?"

He barked out a laugh. "Yes, you're definitely winners!"

"What did I tell you?" Dad exclaimed as he helped Mom and Emmy wipe off the slime.

"So we won?" I asked again. "This is really *The Wheel of Horror*?"

"Huh?" The host shook his head. "What's *The Wheel of Horror*? This is a banquet. Our annual Monster Lodge banquet. And now, it's time for lunch!"

The audience cheered.

"Let's see now — you said you'd rather be baked than fried, right?" the emcee asked.

"I don't understand," Dad told him. "You mean this isn't a game show?"

The emcee shook his head.

"Then why did we have to do all that in the hotel?" Dad demanded. "What was that all about?"

"Well, we've found that people *taste* better when they're scared," the emcee explained. "I guess being scared gets the juices flowing or something." His teeth gleamed. "Anyway, I'm sure you're going to be delicious!"

An icy shiver ran up my spine. This guy is serious! I realized. The snakes, the elevator guy, the horrible ghouls — they're all real! This is no game!

The emcee waved his arm, and the black-haired woman appeared, rolling a table in front of her. She wore a big white paper bib, the kind that usually has a lobster drawn on it.

But this bib had a drawing of a human being on it.

She rolled the table to a stop. On it sat a big wooden bowl with a bunch of torn-up bread inside it.

I pointed to the bread. "What's that for?"

"Stuffing!" The emcee licked his lips. "Bread stuffing. You don't think we'd bake you without stuffing you first — do you?"

He licked his lips again. She smiled. Saliva dripped from her mouth.

Both of them took a step toward us across the stage. Then another step.

Dad grabbed Emmy and me and spun us around. "Run!" he cried. He shoved us toward Mom. "Run!"

11

With Mom in the lead, we all took off.

We ran halfway across the stage — into the hairy arms of the two ghouls from the swimming pool.

Their red eyes glowed furiously as they grabbed us with their meaty hands. Snapping their sharp teeth, they shoved us back toward the emcee.

"Hey — we didn't order dinner *to go*!" he chuckled. "Stick around, folks. Things are just about to get really *hot*! We've got a hungry crowd here."

As the crowd roared, I stared out at them. Every one of them wore a paper bib. A bib with a human being on it.

My knees quivered. My heart thundered in my ears. "Please!" I cried. "Please let us go! We thought this was a TV show. We're in the wrong place!"

"Don't worry about it." The emcee patted my shoulder. "You'll be delicious. Really. The oven has been preheated."

He waved his arm. A curtain rose.

Behind it stood a huge oven. Gleaming steel. Industrial strength. Big enough to roast a *moose*!

Or a family of four.

I squeezed my eyes shut. This can't be happening, I thought.

"Thanks for being such good guests," the emcee said. "And now we want you to stay for lunch! Ha-ha!" He waved his arm again, and the black-haired woman pulled open the oven door.

A blazing fire raged inside. Flames licked up from the gleaming steel.

My heart flipped over again. *We're toast!*

I glanced around in a panic. The two ghouls stood behind us. The skeleton creature stood on one side of the stage. The elevator operator waited on the other side.

No way out! I thought. No escape!

Snarling eagerly, the two ghouls began herding us toward the oven.

I could hear the roar and crackle of the flames.

I could feel the heat on my skin.

Go ahead and scream, I told myself. It doesn't matter now. Scream your head off!

I opened my mouth to scream, but no sound came out.

I turned in panic to the rest of my family. They couldn't make a sound, either.

We were all too scared to scream.

In terrified silence, we moved toward the oven.

12

The flames leaped out the oven door.

The heat burned my face.

I *had* to scream. I took a deep breath.

"Congratulations!" the emcee shouted. "You're our new champions!"

Huh? I turned around.

The audience was on its feet, cheering. The ghouls and the other monsters clapped and grinned at us.

"You didn't scream!" the host cried. "You're our winners! Congratulations!"

I gaped at him in disbelief.

The emcee laughed. "It's true," he assured us. "You — the Banks family — are the new winners on *The Wheel of Horror*!"

The audience cheered again. He shook our hands. The ghouls and monsters patted us on the back.

"Whoa!" I cried. "You mean it really *is* the game show?"

"Of course it is!" Dad replied. He gave us all a hug. "What did I tell you?"

Mom smiled and hugged him back. Emmy and I sighed in relief.

The black-haired woman closed the oven door. She handed the host a piece of paper. He held it out toward us. "This is a check made out to you for *one hundred thousand dollars*!"

The audience clapped and cheered.

"Now," he went on. "Would you like to take your winnings — or risk it all next week in our Challenge Round?"

Dad snatched the check and stuffed it in his shirt pocket. "We'll take our winnings."

Thank goodness, I thought. *No way* did I want to go through the Challenge Round.

"But we'll also take our lunch now," Dad added.

"Huh?" the emcee frowned. "What do you mean?"

"It's simple — we want lunch," Dad explained. "We're *very* hungry!"

I sighed. I was kind of hoping Dad wouldn't do this. I mean, it's kind of embarrassing.

But after all that excitement, I was starving. My stomach rumbled loudly. I knew that the game had made my whole family hungry.

I grinned at the emcee.

My fangs slid down over my bottom lip. Razor sharp. Perfect for chewing.

My claws popped out. Long claws. Excellent for slicing.

"Let's eat!" Mom cried.

"Let's eat!" Dad agreed.

And all four of us pounced on the emcee.

We didn't even bother with the stuffing.

Teenage Sponge Boys from Outer Space

# Introduction

SLIM: Hey, Lefty — I washed the car with that new sponge you bought. But it didn't soak up the water very well.

LEFTY: Sponge? What sponge?

SLIM: You know. The big gray one.

LEFTY: Gray one? That wasn't a sponge. That was my cat!

SLIM: No wonder! I thought it was awfully noisy for a sponge!

RIGHTY: I suppose the next story is about a *really scary* sponge?

SLIM: No. It's about some really scary aliens from another planet. It's called *Teenage Sponge Boys from Outer Space*. Want to know the moral of the story?

LEFTY: What?

SLIM: Stay away from guys who wash the

dishes with their *heads*! Dirk and Deke are the alien sponge boys in this story. They're definitely a little soft in the head. But as Mac and Becky find out, the sponge boys can get very scary — if they decide to put the *squeeze* on you. . . .

1

"Where on earth did this come from?" Mom held up a chain with a small plastic ball dangling from the end.

Uh-oh. I knew exactly where it came from.

I also knew something else — I was in trouble. Again.

I like taking things apart. Just for fun.

The problem is — I'm not very good at putting stuff back together. Sometimes I leave something out. Like the chain with the ball that Mom was holding up.

"Okay, Mac. Where does this come from? What did you destroy this time?" Mom sighed.

"I'll put it back, Mom. When I get home from school. And it will be as good as new. I promise."

"WHAT will be as good as new?" she demanded.

I grabbed my backpack from the kitchen table. "The upstairs toilet. See you later!" I raced out the door before she could start yelling.

I hope she doesn't tell Dad about this, I thought, jogging down our path. I was still in trouble for taking apart the doorbell. Guess what? It doesn't ring anymore.

I wish I was better at putting things back together again. I really do. But I guess it's just not my talent. That's the way I look at it, anyway.

I glanced at my watch to see if I was late for school. I couldn't tell. The minute hand was missing. I had taken my watch apart last week.

I ran to my friend Becky's house — just in case I was late. I pick up Becky every morning on the way to school. We're in the same sixth-grade class.

I like hanging out with Becky. She enjoys watching me take things apart. She thinks it's cool. I guess that's why she's my best friend. But I have to tell you something — Becky is a little weird.

Becky's mom answered the door. I walked in and headed straight for the den. Becky is *always* in the den. She's there in the morning before school. She's there in the afternoon after school.

She'd spend the whole weekend there if her parents would let her.

Why?

Because that's where the TV is.

And that's why Becky is weird.

Don't get me wrong. It's not because she loves watching TV. I know lots of kids who love TV. It's because of *what* she watches.

"Come on, Becky. I think we're late for school."

"I can't leave now." Becky didn't turn to look at me. She brushed her long red hair back from her face. Her big green eyes remained on the thirty-two-inch TV screen. "It's time for the forecast."

Becky loves the Weather Channel. She can watch it for hours and hours at a time — until her eyes glaze over. Then she watches it some more.

Weird — right?

"It's sunny and cool. Just stick your head out the window and you'll see," I told her.

"I know what the weather is here." She glanced away from the TV to roll her eyes at me. Then she quickly turned back. "I've already heard Local on the Eights."

"Local on the Eights? What's that?" I asked.

"It's the local forecast, Mac." She rolled her eyes again. "On the eights — eight minutes after the hour. Then eighteen minutes after the hour, then twenty-eight minutes, then thirty-eight minutes, then —"

"Okay. Okay. I get it," I said.

"Local on the Eights. 'Accurate and dependable,'" Becky recited the Weather Channel slogan.

Now I rolled my eyes. "So why are you watching? What are you waiting for?"

"The National Planner."

"What's *that*?" I asked.

"Shhh — it's coming on now." Becky moved to the edge of the couch, her gaze totally fixed on the TV.

I watched too — as the temperature for every major city in the United States slowly scrolled onto the screen.

In alphabetical order.

"Becky — they're only up to Denver! We don't have time to go through the whole country. We have to get to school!" I grabbed her arm and pulled her off the couch.

Becky slipped a dark green sweatshirt over her head, grabbed her backpack, and we took off.

"We must really be late." I glanced around. "I don't see anyone from our class." We always bump into someone we know on the way to school. But the street was deserted.

We broke into a jog. As we neared the woods that grew behind the school, Becky started to run.

"Hurry up, Mac! Mrs. Mormando will have a fit if we're late!" She raced ahead of me.

I put on some speed and caught up to her. "You know — it's *your* fault that we're late!"

"I'm sorry. But I *have* to watch the Weather Channel. What's here today could be gone tomorrow. But if you watch the Weather Channel — you'll always know what to expect!"

Sometimes Becky is *really* weird.

"I can't wait until this weekend," she started. "A warm front is approaching from the Gulf —"

BOOOOM!

A deafening crash exploded in the woods.

We stopped running.

The ground quaked hard under our feet.

Becky grabbed my arm to keep from falling.

We stood that way for a few minutes, until the ground stopped shaking.

"Oh, wow!" I took a deep breath. "What was that?"

2

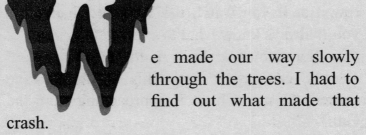e made our way slowly through the trees. I had to find out what made that crash.

Even though the sun was shining, the woods were dark. The branches grew thick and close together, and the fall leaves still clung to them, blocking out the sunlight.

Some of my friends camp out in the woods in the summer. But I don't. I think the woods are kind of creepy.

I led the way, ducking under low branches, pushing them up and away. Peering through the old, gnarled trees. Searching.

"That's strange." I stopped. "Listen."

Becky stood still. Concentrating. "I don't hear anything," she finally said.

"I know. That's what I mean. It's totally silent."

I glanced up into the trees.

I didn't see any birds perching on the branches — or hear their chirping.

I didn't see any squirrels scampering on the limbs — or hear the leaves rustle in their path.

Nothing.

"We should turn back," Becky said. "We're going to be late for school."

"Let's search a little longer," I insisted. "Whatever made a crash that loud can't be hard to find. It's probably something big."

We walked deeper into the woods.

I couldn't find anything.

"We have to go back," Becky declared. "Now!"

"Give me one more second." I started walking fast, darting between the trees. Searching.

Finding — nothing.

I walked faster. Becky kept close behind me.

Then I tripped over a tree root. I stumbled through the trees — into a thick white cloud that billowed through the branches.

Becky hurried up to me. The white cloud swirled around us. Surrounding us.

"That's funny. Local on the Eights didn't

say anything about fog." Becky scratched her head, confused.

"It's not fog. It's smoke," I told her. "We must be getting close! Come on." I raced up ahead.

"Mac, we're definitely going to be late for school," she called after me. "I don't want to get in trouble. I'm heading back."

Becky marched away.

I heard her footsteps slowly fading — but I kept searching.

What crashed? I wondered. It has to be here somewhere!

I zigzagged through the trees — and stopped.

"Becky! Come back!" I cried. "I found it!"

3

"hat is it?" Becky came racing through the woods.

"I don't know. It's over there." I pointed to the trees just ahead of me.

I took a step forward — squinting at the large dark object that stretched out underneath the trees.

Becky marched right up to it.

"Mac! You're not going to believe this!" She reached down and picked something up from the ground.

"What is it?" I ran up to her.

"A pinecone — with its scales open!" she declared.

"So what?" I asked.

"A pinecone with open scales means we're going to have nice weather! When the scales close up, it means rain is on the way. I learned that on *Weather Wise* — a show on the Weather Channel. Isn't it cool?"

"Oh, yeah, really cool," I mumbled.

"Well, it's more interesting than that." She pointed at the dark object under the trees. "That's just an old tent."

I bent down for a close look.

Becky was right.

It was just an old canvas tent. Half-decayed. Covered in a layer of thick moss. It was probably left there by one of my friends last summer or the summer before.

"Come on. We can't search anymore." Becky tugged me away. "We're really late now. We're going to be in major trouble."

We crashed through the trees and ran full speed to school. When we reached our classroom, we peeked inside and saw Mrs. Mormando sitting at her desk, staring down, writing.

We tiptoed to our seats in the middle of the classroom.

We quietly sat down.

Mrs. Mormando didn't glance up.

She didn't see us sneak in.

I gave Becky the thumbs-up sign. Then I opened my notebook — and Mrs. Mormando lifted her head from her work.

"We all have jobs to do." She pushed her chair back. "And one of your jobs is to come to school on time."

Uh-oh.

"Now I want everyone who was late today to stand." Mrs. Mormando glanced around the room.

We didn't stand.

"I can wait." She crossed her arms in front of her. "I know who the two of you are."

Becky glanced at me.

"She knows. We'll have to stand," I whispered to her.

"She *can't* know," Becky whispered back. "She didn't see us."

"She knows!" I insisted. "We have to stand — or we'll be in bigger trouble!"

We stood up.

I could see Becky's lower lip tremble slightly.

"Oh. I didn't know *you* were late *too*." Mrs. Mormando stared at me and Becky. Then she glanced past us — to the back of the room.

Huh?

I turned around — and saw the twins, Dirk and Deke, standing.

Oh, brother. Becky was right — Mrs. Mormando didn't know. We gave ourselves up for nothing!

"The four of you will stay after class and write compositions on *punctuality*. *Punctuality,*" she repeated the word. "That means *being . . . on . . . time.*"

Dirk and Deke lowered their heads, embarrassed.

I felt sorry for them. They were new in school. They had just started in September. They didn't know how strict Mrs. Mormando is.

I felt sorry for them for another reason too. Dirk and Deke were kind of nerdy — and strange looking.

They were really, really skinny. And tall — taller than anyone else in the class. They looked like human string beans. I guess that's what made them look nerdy.

Their skin made them look strange. It was very pale — whiter than chalk. And kind of bumpy.

I didn't really know anything about Dirk and Deke. Nobody in class did. They were both shy. They hadn't made a single friend since they started here.

And now they had to stay late after school.

Bad break for them, I thought. And for us.

"Everyone — step up to the chalkboard," Mrs. Mormando interrupted my thoughts. "I've written a math problem for each of you to solve."

"*Problem* is right," I mumbled, staring at the numbers on the board.

I didn't know what to do. I stared at the example some more.

I glanced next to me — at Becky. Her chalk squeaked across the board fast.

"This is easy!" she whispered, scribbling away.

I watched Becky work on her problem. But I still didn't know how to figure out mine.

I glanced away again — this time across the room, at Dirk.

He wrote some numbers on the board.

Then he leaned forward.

He started to erase what he wrote — and I gasped.

Dirk was erasing the board — *with his head*!

4

irk suddenly jerked his head away from the board. He turned to me. He saw me staring at him.

He narrowed his eyes at me. His mouth turned down. He let out a low growl.

I quickly turned away. I stared at the board in front of me, pretending to study the numbers. But all I could picture was Dirk, erasing the board with his head.

I stole another glance at him.

He was writing again.

He had chalk smeared across his forehead.

That guy is *really* weird! I thought. I turned away quickly before he caught me staring at him again.

"Time's up," Mrs. Mormando announced. She checked our examples. Becky was the only one who solved the example correctly on my side of the room.

On the other side of the room, Dirk and Deke were the only ones who got it right.

"I bet Dirk and Deke are really smart," Becky said to me on the way to lunch.

"Those guys are kind of strange," I said. "I saw Dirk erasing the board —"

"It's not strange to be good in math, Mac," Becky interrupted me. "I think you're jealous of them."

"Jealous of *them*! You've got to be kidding! All I was trying to say is — Dirk is a little strange. He was erasing the board —"

"Strange?" Becky interrupted me again. "*You* like to take things apart! Some people might think you're strange. Did you ever think of that?"

We turned into the cafeteria. Becky sat down and threw her books on a table.

"I'll save our spots here," she said. "It's your fault that we have to stay late today — so you get the drinks."

I shook my head as I walked across the cafeteria to the food line. Sometimes Becky can be a real pain.

I bought a hot dog and two cans of soda and started to make my way back to our table.

"Throw it!" Becky called from across the

room. She held her hands up, ready to catch the can of soda.

I swung my arm back and aimed for Becky.

The can slipped from my grip.

Instead of sailing high across the room, it flew straight out in front of me.

I inhaled sharply — and watched with dread as it crashed right into Deke's skull.

5

The can of soda hit Deke — and bounced off his head.

I stood frozen, waiting for him to cry out in pain. But he didn't cry out. He didn't make a sound. He didn't utter a word. He didn't even touch his head to see if he had a bump.

He gave the can a casual glance as it crashed to the floor. Then he gazed up — and glared at me. His face twisted into a deep scowl.

"Hey, Deke —" I started to apologize, and the skin on his face tightened. The bumps on his cheeks popped out and turned bright red.

I started to apologize again. But I changed my mind when Deke let out a low grunt.

These guys are too weird, I thought.

I walked away as fast as I could, but not too fast. I didn't want to look as if I was running.

"Did you *see* that, Becky?" I dropped down next to her. My heart raced. "Did you see the can of soda bounce off Deke?"

"Yeah," she answered. "He must have a really hard head!"

"Can't you move a little faster?" Becky walked a few steps ahead of me on our way home from school.

We had stayed late after school to write our essays on punctuality. Becky was still annoyed with me.

"My fingers hurt from all that writing." She shook her hand. "Ten pages of writing . . . writing . . . writing about why it's important to be on time."

"I already said I'm sorry. Can't we talk about something else?" I pleaded.

Becky didn't answer me, so we walked in silence.

"I saw a great program on TV the other night," she finally said.

"What was it?" I asked, relieved that she was talking to me again.

"It was called *Spring Fever and Other Weather Diseases*. It was a special program on the Weather Channel. It was all about how the weather affects our bodies."

116

"Can't we talk about something else?" I begged.

"No." She glared at me.

I let out a sigh.

"Did you know the sun can make you sneeze?" she went on.

I nodded yes, even though I didn't know that. I wasn't even sure I believed it.

"Okay. Did you know that a falling barometer can give you a headache?" she asked.

I didn't know a falling barometer could give me a headache. I *did* know Becky could.

"Sure," I lied. "Everyone knows that."

"Did you know that your heart beats faster when the temperature drops quickly?" Becky kept at it.

"Of course," I lied again.

"I don't believe you," she shouted. "You did not know that!"

"He doesn't know anything." I heard a voice in the woods. Dirk stepped out from behind a tree. Deke followed him. They blocked our path.

"That's not true," Becky said to them. "Mac knows a lot of stuff. He just doesn't know anything about the weather. Or about math."

Becky smiled at them.

Dirk and Deke didn't smile back.

They reached out — and grabbed us.

117

Dirk gripped my shoulder.

Deke grabbed Becky by the arm.

"Hey — what are you doing?" I cried. "What's the big idea?"

Dirk and Deke didn't answer. They started walking, pulling us with them.

"I have to get home!" Becky jerked her arm back, trying to yank free. "Let me go!"

I twisted my shoulder, struggling to break Dirk's grip. But he clamped down harder, squeezing his fingers, tightening his hold on me.

"What are you doing?" I yelled again.

"You'll see," Dirk growled.

"Real soon," Deke finished.

Then they shoved us hard toward the trees — and forced us into the woods.

6

Dirk and Deke dragged us deep into the woods.

We tried hard to wrestle free, but for skinny guys, they were strong. Too strong for us.

We yelled and pleaded with them to let us go. They ignored our cries.

Finally, they stopped and released us. "Thanks for coming." Dirk laughed. His laugh sounded like the bray of a donkey.

"Haw. Haw. Haw." Deke laughed too.

"I'm getting out of here," Becky whispered to me. She turned and started to run. But Deke was fast. He took two strides on his long legs, stretched out a long arm, and caught her.

"You can't leave yet." His lips parted into a wide smile. "We have to show you something."

These guys were really strange — and really creepy.

"We'll come back and see it another time," I said lamely.

"NO!" Dirk declared. "We have to show you something now." He turned to Deke. "Are you ready?"

Deke nodded.

The two guys lifted their hands and placed them on the sides of their heads.

Then they pressed their hands down — and squeezed.

Their heads were soft!

They pushed some more — pushed on their mushy heads.

I stared in shock as they squeezed and pinched and molded their skulls.

As their heads shrank, their eyes moved in toward each other. Their noses sank into their faces.

They pressed some more — until they had squeezed their heads into two tiny knots.

Then they lifted their hands — and *NG!* Their heads sprang back out. Their eyes ˀto place. Their noses popped out.

ˀd you see that?" I cried.

ˀth hung open, but no words

"How — how did you do that?" I stammered.

"We're not from your planet," Dirk declared. "We're sponge people."

"Very funny." I rolled my eyes.

"That . . . wasn't . . . a . . . joke," Deke declared. "Look."

Deke led us behind some trees. He stopped in front of something hidden under a thick blanket of branches.

I couldn't tell what was hiding under there — I could only tell that it was big.

Dirk lifted up the branches — and I gasped.

A spaceship!

A real spaceship — shiny silver and shaped like a flying saucer!

"Whoa!" I walked around it. It was the size of a small car, with a circle of blue lights dotting its widest part. It was pretty banged up and badly dented. Some of the lights hung loose.

"Whoa!" I walked around it again. "Whoa!" I couldn't stop saying, "Whoa!"

A spaceship! These guys really were from another planet!

"What happened to it?" Becky pointed to an enormous dent on the spaceship's side.

"We crash-landed on your planet," Deke explained. "We're teenagers. We just got our intergalactic driver's licenses. I guess we were going too fast. And we crashed here."

"Good thing we had air bags," Dirk added.

"We heard a loud crash this morning," Becky said.

"That was us," Dirk declared. "We've been trying to get this thing to fly. We've been working on it for weeks, trying to fix it.

"This morning we tested it. We got up pretty high. Then we crashed back down again."

I listened to Dirk explain. I couldn't believe what I was hearing! Aliens from outer space! And they had landed here, in *our* little town! This was incredible!

We had to tell everyone in school about this. No. Wait. We had to tell the whole world!

"We don't want anyone to know about us," Dirk said as if he could read my mind. His eyes narrowed. "We have to get off your planet. We're sponge life. Our bodies are too soft and squishy for your planet."

"If you don't want anyone to know about you, why are you telling *us*?" I asked.

Dirk stepped up in front of me.

He lowered his big sponge head until it nearly touched my head. "We need help to leave this planet. We went to your school to find kids

122

who could help us. And we picked you — because you were starting to figure things out."

"No — no I wasn't," I stammered, backing away.

"Yes, you were." He stepped forward. "I saw you staring at me in class today."

He poked me hard in the chest, and I stumbled backwards. "You're smart. You were starting to figure things out. I could tell."

"Yeah. You're smart." Deke stepped up and shoved me. "Too smart. Now you have to help us get back home."

"What if we *won't* help you?" Becky asked.

"You'll help us," Dirk insisted.

"How can you be so sure?" Becky pressed on.

I watched in horror as the bumps on Dirk's skin turned bright red and his eyes bulged out.

"You'll help us," he growled, staring deep into Becky's eyes. "You will . . . you will . . ."

7

"I want to go home." Becky shivered in the October night air. "I don't know why we're doing this. We don't have to help them."

Three days had passed since we'd discovered that Dirk and Deke were teenage sponge boys from outer space. Three of the worst days of my life.

Every afternoon after school, they forced us into the woods. Forced us to work on their broken spaceship late into the night.

We brought them nails, hammers, and food. We held up lights so that they could work in the dark woods. They worked until the first rays of morning sun filtered through the trees. Then they let us go home.

Every night I had to sneak out of my house.

124

Then every morning, sneak back in again, before Mom and Dad got up.

I was totally wrecked.

I dragged my feet as Becky and I sneaked around to the back of my house. It was after midnight. Except for the low chirp of a single cricket, the night was silent.

We headed quietly to the garage. I didn't want to wake Mom and Dad. They went to bed really late tonight. I nearly fell asleep, waiting for them to conk out. But they finally did. Then I called Becky and told her it was safe to come over.

"We don't have to help them," Becky repeated. "What can they do to us?"

"I don't know," I whispered. "And I don't want to find out! We're helping them — and that's that. They'll be gone soon — and we won't have to worry about them anymore."

"Soon! How soon is *soon*?" Becky's voice grew louder. "I haven't done my homework in three nights. I'm falling way behind in school! Soon better be *real* soon!"

What could I say?

I felt the same way. I was way behind in my schoolwork too. And I kept falling asleep in class.

But we had no choice.

We had to help Dirk and Deke. I was afraid

of them. I wanted them to leave, fast. And if that meant helping them, that's what I was going to do. Even if I had to steal the battery out of my dad's car, which is exactly what I was going to do tonight.

The sponge boys said their spaceship was ready for liftoff. They had everything they needed — except for the power supply.

I didn't know if the car battery would work in their spaceship. I wasn't sure if it could power their craft.

I prayed it would. Then I could say goodbye to them forever!

I lifted the garage door slowly. I raised it up inch by inch, careful not to make a sound.

"It's too dark in here," Becky complained. "How are we supposed to see?"

"No problem." I took a flashlight out of my back pocket. "Hold this while I lift the hood." I handed the light to Becky.

I released the lock on the hood, and it popped open.

I felt around for the wrench in my other back pocket. Then I started to loosen the bolts that held the battery in place.

"If your dad catches you doing this, you're going to be in major trouble," Becky warned.

"Gee, thanks, Becky. I didn't realize that."

Becky shrugged.

It's a good thing I'm great at taking things apart, I thought. I loosened the cables.

"That should do it." I turned to Becky. "I'm ready to take the battery out. Here." I held the wrench out to Becky.

She reached for it. But I let it go before she had it. It clanged loudly on the cement floor — and a light flashed on in my parents' bedroom.

"Oh, nooo!" I moaned. "We're caught!"

8

"Maybe they'll go back to bed." I stood frozen, staring up at my parents' bedroom window, praying their light would go out.

The back porch light flashed on.

I quickly lowered the car hood.

Becky ducked behind a fender. "Don't let him see me," she whispered. "I don't want to get in trouble too."

"Who's out there?" Dad demanded, poking his head out the back door.

"It's — it's just us," I answered. "Just Becky and me."

Becky kicked me in the leg as she stood up.

"What on earth are you doing out there? Do you know what time it is?" Dad asked. "Becky, do your parents know you're out this late?"

"Uh — her parents know," I answered. "They said it's okay. Because we're, um, doing our astronomy homework."

"Yeah," Becky added. "We have to draw a star chart."

Dad gazed up into the night sky. "How are you going to do that? Look at all those heavy clouds. You can't see a single star shining out there tonight."

"We know," I said quickly. "Our teacher told us to use our imagination."

"Well, you should have told me you were going to be out so late," Dad said. "You scared your mom and me to death."

"Sorry, Dad. I — I didn't remember the assignment until it was too late. You and Mom were already asleep. I'm really sorry."

"Okay. But don't stay out too much longer." He went back inside.

I stared up at my parents' bedroom, waiting for Dad to shut off the light. As soon as it went out, I carefully lifted the hood of the car.

I reached inside for the battery. I tried to lift it — but I couldn't. "I need help, Becky. The battery is rusted in place. It's stuck."

"How am I supposed to help if I have to hold the light?" she asked.

"Becky!"

"This is stupid," she grumbled. "I'm tired of working day and night. I'm never going to help you again." She tucked the flashlight under her arm and reached into the car.

"You won't have to help me again," I told her as we tugged on the battery. "When my dad sees the battery missing, he'll probably kill me!"

We tugged and tugged — and the battery finally came loose.

Becky closed the garage door — and we headed for the woods to meet the sponge boys.

It was cold in the woods. Cold and damp. And dark.

No stars shone above. No moonbeams filtered through the trees. The heavy clouds blocked out any twinkle of light.

Becky swept the flashlight beam in front of us so we could find our way.

A wind picked up. It whistled through the trees. I shivered.

What if the battery doesn't work? A chill swept through my whole body. *What if the sponge boys put it in their spaceship and nothing happens? What will they do to us?*

9

"**W**hat took you so long?" Dirk scowled at me.

He and Deke stood beside the spaceship. A battery-powered lamp that I "borrowed" from Dad hung over a tree branch. Dirk and Deke stood in its bright circle of light.

They looked really creepy in the yellow beam. The bumps in their skin appeared larger and took on a greenish glow. But the spaceship looked awesome.

Dirk and Deke had knocked out all the bangs and dents. And Becky and I had really shined it up. It sparkled.

"The battery was stuck." My voice sounded loud in the still of the night. "And my dad caught us," I whispered.

"You didn't tell him about us — did you?" Deke asked, moving in on me.

"Of course he didn't," Becky declared. "Here — take this." She grabbed the battery out of my hands and shoved it into Deke's chest.

Deke stumbled backwards.

Dirk took the battery.

"Now you have what you want." Becky planted her hands on her waist. "So let us go. I have to get some sleep tonight."

"Sorry. We can't let you go." Dirk stared down at the battery in his hands. "I've never seen a power supply like this one before. You're going to have to hook it up."

"No problem," Becky said. "Mac will do it."

Uh-oh.

"I — I can't," I stammered.

"Just do it, Mac. So we can get out of here," Becky declared. "I'm tired."

Deke grabbed me tightly by the shoulders. He breathed in my face, and I nearly gagged from the smell of his sour breath.

"Put in the power source — or you'll never sleep again." He shook my shoulders hard.

"You don't understand," I tried to explain. "I'm not very good at putting things together. I never do it right. Our toilet still doesn't flush."

"What's a toilet?" Deke asked me.

"Well, it's, um —"

"Stop wasting time," Dirk cut me off. "Put this thing in — or else!"

"Or else what?" Becky asked. "I'm tired of all your threats. I'm tired of you bossing us around. Or else what?" she demanded.

I wanted to strangle Becky.

I watched in fear as Dirk's eyes narrowed into two tiny slits. He placed the battery on the ground.

My heart began to pound as he straightened up and reached out for me.

He grabbed my hand — and jerked it roughly toward him. Then he wrapped his fingers around mine.

He closed his eyes. And squeezed his fingers tightly. He squeezed my hand so hard, his knuckles started to turn white.

I waited to feel the pain. I waited for it to shoot through my hand and up my arm.

But I didn't feel anything. I glanced over at Becky and shrugged my shoulders.

Dirk uncurled his fingers. A slow smile spread across his lips. "Look," he said, gazing at my hand.

I glanced down — and screamed.

"I'm a sponge!" I cried out in horror. "He turned my fingers into sponges!"

133

I raised my hand — and watched my fingers flop in the air.

I touched them.

My skin didn't feel like skin. My bones were gone!

My fingers felt soft and squishy — like sponges!

"Ohhh," I let out a low moan of terror.

Becky rushed over to me. She squeezed my hand. My wrist. They were still solid.

"If you don't help us, I won't stop at your fingers!" Dirk turned to Becky. "Or yours!" Then he reached out for my head!

"Okay! Okay!" I yelped. "We'll help you! But, please, please turn my fingers back. I'll need them to work. Please!"

Dirk clapped his hands twice sharply. "They're back," he announced.

I glanced down.

I wiggled my fingers.

They didn't flop around. They were solid again.

I lifted the battery from the ground and slowly approached the spaceship. "Um — where exactly does it go?"

"In here." Dirk opened a hatch on the side of the ship. Hundreds of colored wires and cables sprang out.

Oh, boy. I am in big trouble, I thought as I studied the wiring. If this were a car, I'd have a problem putting the battery back in. And this was nothing like a car!

Beads of sweat formed on my forehead as I tried to figure out what do to.

Becky sat against a tree, staring up through the branches. Dirk and Deke stood behind me. Watching me.

I inched forward, away from them. I didn't want either one of them to touch me. Even by accident.

I stared into the hatch. Here goes, I thought. I connected half of the wires and cables to one side of the battery. The other half to the other side.

"All done," I said.

"Great!" Becky jumped up from the ground. "Let's go! Have a nice trip!" She grabbed my hand and started to tug me away.

"NOT YET!" Dirk's voice boomed through the night.

We froze.

"First, you have to help us with the final inspection," he ordered. His voice softened. "And you want to watch us blast off, don't you?"

I didn't want to be anywhere near here when the sponge boys tried to take off. But I

135

knew Dirk wasn't really giving us a choice. I let out a sigh. "Sure."

Becky and I took a seat in the spaceship. "Wow! Look at all these switches and lights!" I stared at the control panel in awe.

I'd never seen so many gadgets in such a small space. It was amazing!

Dirk and Deke told us which switches to flip. Then they checked the outside lights and the wiring in the hatch.

"Okay. I think we're ready," I heard Dirk tell Deke.

Becky and I stood up.

"Oh, we almost forgot," Dirk said, moving toward us.

"Stop!" I cried. "Don't turn us into sponges. Please!"

"We're not going to do that," Dirk replied. "You helped us. You're our friends. There's just one thing we forgot to mention."

"What's that?" Becky asked.

"We're taking you with us," he answered.

10

"**N**o way! No, you're not!" I jumped out of the spaceship. Becky leaped out too. We tried to run — but the sponge boys blocked our path.

"Get out of our way!" Becky demanded. "We helped you. Now let us go!"

"Sorry," Dirk replied. "But you're coming with us. We can't leave you behind to tell every-one about our visit."

"Get inside," Deke ordered. "Have you ever flown in outer space?"

Becky and I shook our heads no.

"Don't you want to be the first kids on Earth to fly in a spaceship?" he asked.

Becky and I shook our heads no.

"Even if I let you work the controls?" he added.

"We can't do that," I said. "We don't have an intergalactic driver's license."

"That's okay." Deke waved a hand in the air. "We don't, either. We lied to you about that. We just have our learners' permits."

"Enough talk. You're going with us!" Dirk shouted. "So get in!"

Dirk and Deke shoved us toward the spaceship. They pushed us hard, trying to force us inside.

"No. Wait! My shoelace is untied." Becky bent down to tie her sneaker. "Mac, can you help me with this? I have a knot."

She's totally lost her mind, I thought. How can she worry about a knot at a time like this?

I leaned over Becky's sneaker. I didn't see a knot. Becky moved her head close to mine and whispered in my ear, "Stall them. Don't let them get in the ship."

"Huh? Why?"

"Just stall them!" she whispered, then she stood up. "Thanks, Mac. That's better." She turned to the sponge boys. "I hate knots in my laces, don't you?"

Deke let out a short grunt.

"Are you ready?" Dirk snapped.

"Almost," I said. "But, first, I have to stretch. I'm not good at sitting in one spot for a long time. And this is going to be a long ride. Right?"

Dirk and Deke nodded.

"Well, then, I'd better stretch — so my muscles don't get cramped."

"Me too," Becky said.

Becky and I faced each other. "Ready. Begin." I started doing jumping jacks. Becky followed along.

"Okay, now. Hands on hips and bend, bend." Becky and I dipped from side to side.

"Touch your toes! Touch your toes! For eight counts. Here goes!" I cheered, and we touched our toes — up and down eight times.

The sponge boys leaned against a tree, watching us. Dirk let out a loud grunt.

"Why don't you join us?" I suggested.

"Yeah," Becky said. "You should stretch your muscles before such a long flight."

"Okay. Time to raise our arms high," I said, lifting my arms over my head.

"Streeetch! Streeetch!" Becky stretched her arms way up. "Streeetch it out! Reach for the moon!"

"That's enough!" Dirk moved away from

the tree. "Enough stretching. Get inside now!" He pointed to the spaceship.

"We've got to keep them here," Becky whispered to me. "Just a little bit longer."

"It's no use, Becky." My voice trembled. "I can't stall anymore. I don't know what else to do!"

11

"No more fooling around." Deke guided Becky and me to the spaceship. "It's time to go!"

"Okay. Okay. We're ready," Becky said. "Just one more minute. We just want to say good-bye to Earth."

Becky stared at the branches overhead. "Good-bye trees. Good-bye leaves. Good-bye woods."

"Good-bye rocks. Good-bye dirt," I added.

"Good-bye school. Good-bye Mrs. Mormando. Good-bye homework," she went on.

"Good-bye Mom," I continued. "Good-bye Dad —"

A lightning bolt exploded in the dark sky. I could see Becky's smile in the bright flash.

A clap of thunder boomed. It started to rain.

I felt a few light drops on my face. Then another flash of lightning — and it started to pour.

We were drenched in seconds.

"I knew it!" Becky cheered. "I knew it would rain! I knew those were stratocumulus clouds!"

"Huh?"

"Stratocumulus clouds. Rain clouds!" she told me.

"Oh, nooooo!" the sponge boys moaned. "The rain! Stop! Stop!" Dirk cried out, clutching his head.

We watched in amazement as the sponge boys' heads soaked up the rain — and began to swell.

The more it rained, the larger their heads grew.

"Can't — can't think," Deke groaned. His head had swelled to the size of a watermelon.

"Can't move." Dirk collapsed to the ground, clutching his melon-size head.

"You're a genius, Becky!" I cheered.

"I knew if we just kept them here long enough . . ." Becky stared up at the sky. "We'd better get rid of them now. Before the rain stops and they dry up."

We hoisted up the sponge boys, one at a time, and shoved them into their spaceship.

I reached over to the control panel.

I turned on the ignition.

I slammed the top hatch shut.

The spaceship began to rumble. A thin stream of gray smoke escaped from the bottom. Then its blue lights flashed on.

I held my breath as the spaceship shook on the ground, from side to side.

BOOM!

With a loud roar, the ship lifted off the ground. It flew straight up — above the treetops.

The rain poured down on our faces as Becky and I stood and watched the ship soar up, up, up. Soon its blue lights grew faint, and it disappeared into the dark clouds.

"We did it!" I cheered. "We got rid of Dirk and Deke!" I jumped up and down, twisting left and right, swinging my arms high in the air.

I was so happy!

Becky ran circles around the trees, whooping and hollering.

I glanced up at the sky one last time before we left the woods. It was totally dark. "Come on, Becky. Let's go home!"

Becky guided us through the woods with the beam of our flashlight. We ran through the trees as fast as we could — and burst out onto the street.

We didn't stop running until we reached my house. "Bye!" Becky took off for her house.

I slipped quietly in through our back door — and met Mom in the kitchen.

"Mac, I was just coming out to get you! It's really late! Did you finish your astronomy homework?"

"Yes!" I cheered. "We finished!" I was so happy. The sponge boys were gone! Gone for good!

"What's that?" Mom pointed to a shiny bolt I held in my hand.

"Oh." I stared down at it. I didn't even realize I had been holding it. A bolt from the spaceship.

"It's nothing," I told Mom.

I tossed the bolt into the trash — just as a bright blue light came swooping down through the kitchen window.

Then we heard a deafening crash from out in the woods.

"Oh, no!" I moaned. I stared at the bolt at the bottom of the trash can. "Oh, noooooo!"

SNEAK PREVIEW

You'll never guess
what R.L. Stine
has in store for you...

13

The cat jumped to its feet. It arched its back. Pulled back its lips in a menacing hiss. Prepared to attack again.

"No —!" I uttered a sharp cry of protest. Holding my leg, I spun around and frantically hobbled across the wet grass toward the house.

The pain didn't fade. It soared up from my wounded leg. My head throbbed.

In the house, I turned and squinted back across the silvery lawn. The cat hadn't moved. It stood glaring at me with those evil yellow eyes.

With a shudder, I slammed the back door.

Then, holding my leg, I pulled myself up the stairs to the bathroom.

I clicked on the light. Staggered to the sink. Grabbed up a handful of tissues to press against the scratch and stop the bleeding.

I bent over. Lowered the tissues to the wound — and gasped in surprise.

It wasn't bleeding.

The deep scratch marks were a bright white, so bright they appeared to glow.

The scratches cut through the skin — but no blood seeped out. No blood at all.

The next morning, I stood at the kitchen counter, eating my breakfast. Sunlight poured in from the window, sending splashes of yellow around the room. The back door was open. I heard children laughing and shouting somewhere down the block.

Despite the cheerful day, I felt tired and gloomy. I couldn't stop thinking about Rip.

"It's not an ordinary cat." Crystal's frightened words came back to me. *"You shouldn't have messed with Rip."*

I swallowed down my breakfast hungrily. Standing at the counter, I shuddered when I thought of the cat covering my face as I slept.

What was it trying to do?

Was it really trying to smother me?

I pictured it sailing out the window. I remembered the hard *thud* as it landed on the ground two stories below.

It died. But it didn't die.

"Mom — I've really got to talk to you!" I shouted.

"Alison, you don't have to shout." She startled me. She was standing a few feet away, in the kitchen doorway.

"Mom —" I started.

But her eyes were on the counter. Her face filled with alarm. "Alison — what on earth are you doing?" she cried. "What kind of breakfast is *that*?"

I looked down — and let out a startled cry. "Oh no. I don't believe it!"

I stared in horror at the empty cans on the kitchen counter.

I had gobbled down three cans of tuna, right from the can.

felt a little better by play rehearsal time after school that afternoon. I didn't have my usual energy. But at least I didn't feel so shaky and weird.

I just need a good night's sleep, I decided. I need a night without a mysterious cat climbing over my face. I made my way down the rows of auditorium seats and climbed onto the stage.

Ryan and Freddy were arm wrestling beside the royal throne in the center of the stage. Freddy was so much bigger than Ryan, he barely had to strain. Ryan's face was bright red and twisted in pain as Freddy pushed his arm down.

Other kids urged them on, cheering and laughing.

At stage right, kids on the crew were working on the castle balcony. It was actually a tall cardboard cutout, strapped onto the front of a very tall ladder.

In the last act, I had to climb the ladder and lean over the balcony as I talked with Ryan. I'd already tested the ladder a few times. It was kind of shaky.

I don't like heights to begin with. Climbing up there made me really nervous. But Mr. Keanes promised that the ladder would be solidly anchored.

"Just watch your step as you climb it," he told me, "and you'll be perfectly fine."

I dropped my backpack at the side of the stage. Then I walked over to the throne.

As I approached, Freddy slammed Ryan's hand down hard on the throne arm. Freddy jumped up, raising both hands over his head in triumph as the other kids cheered.

Still red-faced, Ryan moved away, scowling and shaking his hand in pain.

"Never try to arm wrestle with the *king*!" Freddy called after him.

I hurried over to Ryan. "I think Freddy is starting to take his part in the play too seriously," I said. "Since when does he call himself *king*?"

Ryan shook his hand some more. "He cheated," he muttered. "I almost had him, but he cheated."

I couldn't help myself. I laughed. "How do you cheat at arm wrestling?" I demanded.

"By being bigger and stronger than me!" Ryan exclaimed.

We both laughed.

"Where is Mr. Keanes?" I asked.

"He's in the office, talking to some parent," Freddy said, tossing his king's crown from hand to hand. He motioned to the ladder. "Alison, are you ready for the balcony scene?"

I gazed at the tall ladder. The kids on the stage crew were having trouble attaching the cardboard balcony cutout. One of them let out a cry as the whole thing nearly toppled over.

"Maybe we won't do it today," I said. "I haven't had time to learn my lines for that scene."

Freddy turned to Ryan. "How's your hand? I didn't break it, did I?" He grinned.

"It's okay," Ryan replied, scowling. "Next time, I'll give you a few pointers."

"Next time?" Freddy laughed. "You're ready to go again?"

Ryan avoided Freddy's gaze. "Maybe tomorrow," he muttered.

We kidded around for a while, waiting for Mr. Keanes. Down at the seats, some kids in the chorus started to rehearse one of the songs.

The stage crew finally got the balcony hooked onto the ladder. They all climbed down to admire it.

Ryan was talking about a funny thing that happened in Mr. Clay's art class earlier in the afternoon. Ryan does a perfect imitation of Mr. Clay's high, shrill voice.

We were all laughing and trying to sound like Mr. Clay too.

Suddenly, Ryan stopped. His smile faded. He narrowed his eyes at me.

"Alison — what is your problem?" he asked. "Why are you doing that?"

"Weird!" Freddy cried. "Why are you licking the back of your hands?"

I gave the back of my left hand a few more licks. Then I examined both hands. Perfectly clean now.

I dried them on the legs of my jeans.

"Hey —" I demanded. "Why is everyone staring at me?"

15

A short while later, Mr. Keanes finally arrived, and we started to rehearse.

Mr. Keanes seemed more frantic than usual. He kept bouncing around the stage, interrupting us every few seconds, scribbling furiously on his clipboard. After only a few minutes, he had big sweat stains under the arms of his shirt.

I guess he's nervous because the play performance is only a week away, I thought. I felt a little nervous too. How would I ever memorize all my lines by then?

I jumped and spun around when I thought I heard a cat's cry. But it was only the squeak of a chair being opened in the auditorium.

When I turned back, Mr. Keanes was staring at me. "Didn't you hear me Alison?" he asked, peering at me over those round glasses of his. "I said let's try the balcony scene."

"Oh, sorry." I turned and made my way quickly to the ladder at the side of the stage. Mr. Keanes called two boys to come hold it steady for me.

"Here goes," I murmured. I took a deep breath and started to climb.

"How is it?" Mr. Keanes called. "Pretty steady?"

"Yeah. Not bad," I replied. I gripped the sides of the ladder tightly and pulled myself up rung by rung.

Alison, don't look down, I instructed myself.

But, of course I couldn't help it. I glanced down at Ryan, Freddy, and the others in the cast. They were all watching me climb.

I was breathing hard by the time I reached the top. I gripped the edge of the cardboard balcony and peered out.

"How's the weather up there?" Freddy called.

"Not bad!" I shouted down. "It's a little cloudy, but —"

"It's getting late. Let's try the scene," Mr. Keanes interrupted impatiently. "Ryan, take your place."

Ryan scratched his head. "Where do I go?"

Mr. Keanes motioned with the clipboard. "Under the balcony. Yes. That's right. Now, remember, Alison, you're very angry with him. You've just discovered that he's not a prince. He's a fake. And you want to pay him back for tricking you."

"I've got it," I called down from my high perch. "Anger. I'll be angry, Mr. Keanes."

He nodded and motioned for Ryan to start.

But before Ryan could open his mouth, Jenny, one of the secretaries in the principal's office, came running down the center aisle of the auditorium. "Alison! Alison!" she called.

I stared down at her.

"Alison? Phone call for you," she called up to me. "It's your mom."

"Huh? Is everything okay?" I cried.

"Yes. But she said she needs to ask you something — right away," Jenny replied.

"Okay," I told her. "I'm coming right down."

I peered down at the stage floor. Not that far, I told myself. I'll land easily on all fours.

I raised my front paws. Arched my back. Kicked off with my back paws.

And leaped off the top of the ladder.

heard screams from down on the stage.

As I plunged down, I saw the clipboard fall from Mr. Keanes' hands. I saw Ryan's mouth open in shock. He shot out both hands, as if trying to catch me.

I landed hard on my hands and knees on the stage floor.

Pain roared through my body.

I rolled onto my back.

And let out a startled gasp.

Why did I do that? Why on earth did I leap off the top of the ladder?

Was I losing my mind?

"Help her!" someone shrieked.

The auditorium rang out with shrill, frightened cries.

"Did she fall?"

"Did she jump?"

"Is she okay?"

"Somebody — call 911!"

I saw Ryan and Freddy and some of the kids in the stage crew running toward me. But I didn't wait for them. I jumped to my feet and ran off the stage.

I bumped past Jenny and bolted up the aisle.

I heard everyone calling to me. But I didn't stop. I didn't want to answer their questions. I didn't want to tell them why I jumped like that.

Because I *didn't know* why I did it.

I knew I couldn't explain it. I'd been acting so strangely all day. Since breakfast. I hadn't felt right. I hadn't felt like myself.

I knew I had to go somewhere and think about it all. But first I had to find out why Mom was calling me at school.

I burst breathlessly into the principal's office. The phone was off the hook on Jenny's desk. I grabbed it up. "Hi, Mom. It's me," I said breathlessly.

"Alison, why are you so out of breath?" Mom demanded.

"I jumped off the top of a ladder!" I blurted out. "It — it was so strange, Mom. I thought I could land on all fours."

I waited for her to reply. But I could hear

her saying something to Tanner. A few seconds later, she came back on the phone. "Sorry. I didn't hear you. Tanner always interrupts when I'm on the phone. What were you saying, Alison?"

"Uh . . . nothing." I no longer felt like explaining it. "What's wrong?" I asked her. "Why are you calling?"

"I need you to come home and babysit Tanner," Mom replied. "I have to go see your Aunt Emma. Some kind of emergency. You know Emma. She sounded really frantic."

"You want me to come home now?" I asked.

"Please hurry," Mom said. "I don't want to leave Tanner alone. He's in one of his moods."

She sighed. "Poor guy. I think something scared him at school or something. He's been acting so tense."

I didn't really feel like going back into the auditorium. I didn't want to face all the questions from everybody. I was glad to have an excuse to leave.

"I'll be right home," I said.

Mom hurried out as soon as I entered the house. "Make sandwiches or something for dinner," she called to me as she climbed into her car. "I'll try not to be too late."

Tanner was definitely in one of his moods. He sat on the floor in his room, staring at a cartoon show on TV. I tried to chat with him. But he only grunted in reply.

I sat beside him on the floor. He scooted away from me grumpily.

"You just want to watch TV?" I asked.

"Maybe," he replied, not taking his eyes off the screen. Then he turned to me. "Want to watch the rest of that movie? *Cry of the Cat*?"

"No way!" I declared. "That video scared you to death — remember?"

He crossed his arms over his little chest. "Then I'm just going to watch cartoons."

"Fine. Let me know when you're ready for dinner," I told him.

"I don't want dinner," he insisted. "You don't know how to make anything good."

What a grump.

At a little after six, he changed his mind. "What's for dinner?" he asked. "I'm starved."

My stomach was growling too. I had a real craving for a big tunafish sandwich. But as Tanner and I headed to the kitchen, I remembered that I'd finished all the tuna at breakfast.

"Maybe I'll just have a bowl of milk," I murmured.

"Huh?" Tanner stared at me. "Can I have peanut butter and jelly?"

"I guess," I replied.

"Very little jelly," he insisted.

"I know, I know," I groaned. Tanner has rules for everything. If you put too much jelly on the peanut butter, he won't eat the sandwich.

I clicked on the kitchen lights, and we walked over to the food cabinets. I started to ask Tanner if he wanted bread or toast. But something caught in my throat.

I started to cough.

I swallowed hard. And coughed some more.

I had the biggest lump in my throat. I couldn't cough it up.

I sucked in a deep breath — and coughed as hard as I could.

My stomach heaved.

The lump caught in my windpipe. I started to choke. I gasped for air.

Tanner's eyes bulged in fright. He grabbed my hand. "Alison, are you okay?"

I couldn't answer him. I was choking. Wheezing. Trying to cough.

Finally, I bent my whole body back — and heaved.

And coughed up the lump. I felt it slide up my throat and roll onto my tongue.

Breathing hard, I reached into my mouth and pulled it out.

"Ohhh." I uttered a groan of disgust.

A wet, black hairball. As big as a Ping-Pong ball.

I held the disgusting wad of black hair in the palm of my hand and stared at it in horror.

"Yuck! That's so *gross*!" Tanner cried.

I turned away from him. I didn't want him to see how frightened I felt.

What is *happening* to me? I wondered.

I knew it had something to do with that cat. Rip.

"Alison, are you sick?" Tanner asked in a tiny voice.

"I — I don't know," I stammered.

I stared down at the disgusting hairball.

I have to go back to that creepy house, I decided. I have no choice. I have to talk to Crystal. She *has* to tell me what is going on!

17

"Alison didn't put enough peanut butter on my sandwich! And she burned the toast!"

That was Tanner's complaint the second Mom and Dad walked in the door.

"I'm sure she tried her best," Dad said, smiling at me.

"Her best *stinks*!" my brother growled.

I stuck out my tongue at him. "Is Aunt Emma okay?" I asked Mom.

She nodded. "Yes. She's fine."

"I — I have to go out now," I blurted.

Dad checked his watch. "It's nearly eight-thirty."

"I promised Ryan I'd help him rehearse his lines for the play." I didn't like to lie to my parents. But there was no way I could tell them I had to see a strange girl about a cat I'd killed three times.

A few minutes later, I was jogging down Broad Street, picking up speed as I moved downhill. It was a clear, cool night. A pale half moon floated low over the treetops. The grass on the lawns glistened under a wet dew.

Two big, shaggy dogs came loping along the sidewalk. They both gazed up at me as I trotted between them. A van filled with teenagers rumbled past, rock music roaring out of its open windows.

I slowed my pace as Crystal's house came into view. I squinted over the weed-cluttered lawn. Pale gray light seeped from the front window.

"She must be home," I murmured to myself.

My sneakers crunched over the gravel driveway. I heard the soft cries of cats from inside the house. Several dark figures stared out at me from the window.

I took a deep breath and knocked on the front door. A chill ran down my back despite the warmth of the night.

Inside the house, the cat cries grew louder.

I wiped sweat off my forehead with the back of my hand. Then I nervously pushed my hair back with both hands. And knocked again.

My heart pounded as I waited. Would Crystal know how to help me? Would she be able to explain to me what was happening?

Finally, the front door creaked open. Crystal poked her head out from the cold, gray light. She was dressed in a long, black jumper. Even in the dim light, I could see cat hairs all over her dress.

She raised her tired, dark eyes to me. "What do you want?" she demanded sharply.

Not very friendly.

"I — I have to talk to you," I stammered. "Do you remember me? I —"

"I really can't talk now," she interrupted. Cats yowled behind her. A scrawny black and white cat brushed against her legs.

She started to close the door.

"But I need your help," I insisted. "I need to find out —"

She kept her hand on the door handle. "Is it about Rip?" she asked.

I nodded. "Yes. You see —"

She raised her hand to cut me off. "Please — go away!" she cried. Her eyes filled with fear. "Please — I can't!"

I grabbed the door to keep her from slamming it. "You've got to help me!" I screamed. "You've got to explain what's going on."

"No —" she started. Her chin trembled. Her frightened eyes reflected the eerie gray light. "No. Mom is very unhappy. Mom doesn't want me to talk to you."

"But — just listen to me!" I pleaded. "I killed that cat. I know it sounds crazy. But I killed Rip. I killed him *three times*!"

Crystal gasped. She raised her hand to her mouth.

"He — he keeps coming back," I told her. "I killed him, and he came back."

Cats cried inside the house. Crystal leaned closer. The gray light spilled over us. She grabbed my arm. Her hand felt as cold as ice.

"How many times did you kill Rip?" she asked in a whisper.

"Three," I told her. "Three times."

"Noooooooo!" She opened her mouth in a horrified cry. Her cold hand squeezed my arm.

"Why? What's wrong?" I demanded in a trembling voice. "What does that mean?"

"He's used up eight lives," Crystal groaned, shaking her head. "He's used up eight. He'll be desperate now. Be careful. Stay away from him. Rip will be *desperate*."